"Will you kiss me, Jonathan?"

Lisette's throat was tight. "I need to know if we have a spark. I'm not making light of this. It's important to me."

Jonathan's eyes lit with a flame that took her breath away and made her knees go weak. "As you wish," he said quietly.

Carefully, he cupped her neck in two big hands and tilted her head slightly to one side. He found her mouth and covered her lips with his.

"Oh..." Her startled exclamation was involuntary.

He was her boss. She was his assistant. Before today, she would never have dreamed of crossing this line.

Jonathan made a sound low in his throat...a groan. A ragged sigh. "Relax, Lisette."

He dragged her closer, deepening the kiss, pressing her to him, his body responding to hers. His sex thrust against her abdomen.

Pulling back was the correct thing to do. Breaking the connection. Reclaiming sanity.

Neither of them chose to be wise.

This wasn't a fairy tale. She was about to travel a road that ended in disaster...

* * *

A Contract Seduction is part of the
Southern Secrets series.

Dear Reader,

Sometimes we have to make tough decisions under a moment of stress. We might get it right. We might get it wrong. For Jonathan and Lisette, it's a matter of taking one step at a time and ultimately realizing what's most important in life.

Thank you for exploring this sexy, high-stakes trilogy set in Charleston, Southern Secrets.

Happy reading!

Janice Maynard

JANICE MAYNARD

A CONTRACT SEDUCTION

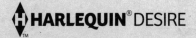

Recycling programs
for this product may
not exist in your area.

ISBN-13: 978-1-335-60365-4

A Contract Seduction

Copyright © 2019 by Janice Maynard

Printed in U.S.A.

www.Harlequin.com

USA TODAY bestselling author **Janice Maynard** loved books and writing even as a child. After multiple rejections, she finally sold her first manuscript! Since then, she has written fifty-plus books and novellas. Janice lives in Tennessee with her husband, Charles. They love hiking, traveling and family time. You can connect with Janice at www.janicemaynard.com, www.Twitter.com/janicemaynard, www.Facebook.com/janicemaynardreaderpage, www.Facebook.com/JaniceSMaynard and www.Instagram.com/TheRealJaniceMaynard.

Books by Janice Maynard

Harlequin Desire

The Kavanaghs of Silver Glen

A Not-So-Innocent Seduction
Baby for Keeps
Christmas in the Billionaire's Bed
Twins on the Way
Second Chance with the Billionaire
How to Sleep with the Boss
For Baby's Sake

Southern Secrets

Blame It On Christmas
A Contract Seduction

Texas Cattleman's Club: Houston

Hot Texas Nights

Visit her Author Profile page at Harlequin.com, or janicemaynard.com, for more titles.

You can find Janice Maynard on Facebook, along with other Harlequin Desire authors, at Facebook.com/harlequindesireauthors!

For Charles, my one and only—thank you for being my hero in every way!

One

Tumor. Inoperable. Cancer.

Jonathan Tarleton gripped the steering wheel, white knuckled, and stared unseeingly through the windshield. The traffic on the 526 beltway that surrounded Charleston was light in the middle of the day. Even so, he probably shouldn't be driving. He was undoubtedly in shock. But all he could think about was going home.

Like an injured animal seeking its den, he needed to go to ground. To hide. To come to grips with the unimaginable.

Thank God, his sister was recently married and living with her new husband, Jonathan's best friend. If Jonathan had come face-to-face with Mazie at the big house out at the beach, his sibling would have known instantly that something was wrong. The two of them were close.

Under ordinary circumstances, neither Jonathan nor Mazie would still be living under the roof where they had grown up. But their father was all alone and getting more and more feeble day by day. Though a number of the old man's friends had moved to communities where they had companionship and medical care close at hand, Gerald Tarleton clung to his fortress of a home on a barrier island.

Jonathan pulled into the under-house parking and rested his forehead on his hands. He felt weak and scared and angry. How the hell was this going to work? He was the sole force that directed the family shipping company. Even though his father's name was still on the letterhead, Jonathan carried the weight of the entire enterprise.

His twin brother should have been here to help, but Hartley was nowhere to be found. After inexplicably stealing a million dollars from the company and then vanishing, Hartley had been written out of the will and out of their lives.

The betrayal had cut Jonathan to the bone. It was a secret hurt that ate at him like the disease in his body. He and his father were the only ones who knew what had happened. They hadn't wanted to break Mazie's heart or tarnish her image of her big brother.

With a shaking hand, Jonathan turned off the ignition. Instantly—now that the AC was unavailable—humidity began to filter into the vehicle. Jonathan was a South Carolina lowlander to the bone, but the summer heat could be brutal.

He gathered his things and headed upstairs. Because of security concerns, the Tarletons had two high-tech offices inside the house in addition to those at Tarleton

Shipping headquarters. Not only did the arrangement ensure privacy when necessary, but it meant that Jonathan could keep tabs on his father. The situation sometimes cramped his style, but he had a condo in the city where he could escape on occasion.

For a man of thirty-one, almost thirty-two, his social life was a joke. He dated occasionally, but few women understood the demands he juggled. His family's decades-old shipping empire was both his great privilege and his curse. He couldn't even remember the last time he'd felt close to any woman, physically or otherwise.

But he made the sacrifices willingly. He was proud of what the Tarletons had built here in Charleston. Proud, and absolutely determined to see it thrive.

He paused for a moment in the living room to stare out through the expansive plate-glass windows to the ocean glittering beneath a June sun. The view never failed to soothe him. Until today.

Now, the immensity and timelessness of the sea mocked him. Humans were little more than specks in the cosmos. Grains of sand on the immense sandy beach of the infinite universe.

All the old clichés were true. Facing one's mortality turned everything upside down. *Time*, that nebulous resource that once seemed a cheap commodity, was suddenly more precious than anything he had ever stored in a bank vault.

How long did he have? The doctor said six months. Maybe more. Maybe less. How was Jonathan going to tell his sister? His father? What would happen to the company, his family's legacy? Mazie had her own interests, her own life.

She would be the sole owner of the family business

once Jonathan and Gerald were gone. Since she had never shown any signs that she was interested in being a hands-on partner in Tarleton Shipping, maybe she would sell. Perhaps that would be for the best. The end to an era.

The thought pained him more than he could say. Until today he hadn't realized exactly how much he was emotionally invested in the company. It wasn't merely a job to him. It was his birthright and a symbol of his family's place in Charleston's history.

Moments later, he found Gerald Tarleton dozing in a chair in the den. Jonathan didn't wake his father. He felt raw and out of control. And his head hurt like hell.

The debilitating headaches had started almost a year ago. At first they were infrequent. Then the episodes increased. One doctor said it was stress. Another wrote it off as migraines.

A dozen medications had been tried and discarded. Today his doctor had given him a handful of sample pills, along with a prescription for more. Right now Jonathan could take one, climb into bed and hopefully sleep off the throbbing pain.

But that wouldn't solve the bigger problems.

The prospect of drugged oblivion was almost irre-sistible. He didn't want to face another minute of this wretched day. But when he reached the kitchen, he grabbed a tumbler, filled it with tap water and downed a couple of over-the-counter acetaminophen tablets.

He had responsibilities. Responsibilities that weren't going anywhere. The only thing that had changed was the time line.

Jonathan always thrived under pressure. Give him a project, a deadline, and he would leap into motion.

The adrenaline rush of achieving the impossible drove him to labor, to excel, to work harder than he had to.

Those traits would stand him in good stead for the next few months.

Grimly he leaned his hip against the marble countertop. In that instant, he made his first postdiagnosis decision. He would keep this news under wraps for now. There was no reason for his family and friends to be upset. To grieve. There would be plenty of time for that when he was gone. Right now, all he wanted was to preserve the status quo.

The first order of business was to make a plan. He would figure this out. Vague, desperate ideas flitted through his brain, each one more flawed or untenable than the last. There had to be an answer. He couldn't simply walk off into that final great sunset and let everything sink into ruin.

He needed time to process, to come to terms with the sword of Damocles hanging over his head. His money and power and influence were worthless currency now. He couldn't buy his way out of this…

Lisette Stanhope punched in the alarm code, waited for the large gates to slide back and then drove slowly onto the Tarleton property. Even after working with Jonathan Tarleton for six years, she never failed to appreciate the magnificence of his family home.

Tarletons had lived for decades on the tip of a small barrier island just north of the city. Their fifteen acres were more than enough for the compound that included the main house and several smaller buildings scattered around.

An imposing gated iron fence protected the enclave

on land. Water access was impossible due to a high brick wall at the top of the sand. The beach itself was public property, but no one could wander onto Tarleton property, either out of curiosity or with dangerous motives. Hurricanes and erosion made the wall outrageously expensive to maintain, but the current Tarleton patriarch was by nature paranoid and suspicious, so security was a constant concern.

When she saw Jonathan's car parked beneath the house, her heart sank. He was usually not home this time of day. She'd been hoping to slip in, say hello to Gerald and put the envelope in her purse on Jonathan's desk.

She could have carried out her errand at the main office where she worked most of the time, but this particular scenario demanded privacy. The decision to turn in her resignation had her stomach in knots. Jonathan would be either furious or perplexed—or both.

After reading her brief note, he would demand an explanation. Naturally. She had been practicing her speech. *In a rut. New challenges. More time to travel.* When she said the words in front of her bathroom mirror, they almost seemed believable. The part that made her wince was acknowledging how good Jonathan and his family had been to her.

Lisette's mother had suffered a debilitating stroke when Lisette was in grad school. For almost seven years, Lisette had worked two jobs and barely managed to keep food on the table and pay the stable of women who helped care for her mother's considerable needs.

Being hired by Tarleton Shipping six years ago had literally changed her life. The generous salary and benefits package had relieved her financial worries to a great extent and had enabled her to spend quality time with her mother.

When her mom had a second stroke and passed away last fall, Jonathan had insisted that Lisette take ample time to mourn and to handle her mother's affairs. Not many other bosses in a corporate setting would have been so generous.

And now Lisette was about to repay Jonathan's immense consideration by abandoning the company…by abandoning her boss.

He wouldn't see this coming, but it was her only choice.

She wanted marriage—a husband and a baby and a normal, ordinary life. Mooning over her boss for another year or two or five was never going to bring those dreams to fruition. She'd had a silly crush on Jonathan, but he'd never once given any indication that he felt the same. She needed a fresh start, a new setting, a chance to meet another man and get Jonathan out of her system once and for all. Her personal life had been on hold for so long she barely knew how to begin, but she knew instinctively that she had to move on.

Her heart slugged in her chest. She didn't want to face him. Guilt and other messier emotions might derail her plan.

When she opened the door at the top of the stairs, again with a code punched in, she stepped into a house that echoed with quiet. Maybe Jonathan wasn't here after all. Maybe a friend had picked him up. Or maybe he was with Mazie and J.B. The newlyweds loved entertaining.

Finding Gerald Tarleton dozing in his favorite recliner was no surprise. Lisette tiptoed past, careful not to wake him. Perhaps if Jonathan was gone or at least upstairs, she could slip in and out without a confrontation.

The upper levels were the family's living quarters. At the back of the main floor, overlooking the driveway, were two rooms that had been outfitted with every conceivable feature to make the offices here as good as or better than the ones downtown.

The smaller of the two was Lisette's domain. She had started out with Tarleton Shipping in accounting but quickly moved up the food chain until she became Jonathan's executive assistant, a title she had held for the past three years. Her job was to do anything and everything to make his life run more smoothly.

And she was good at it. Very good.

A quick visual exploration confirmed that no one was in either office. Now that she was here, her misgivings increased tenfold. She reached into her purse for the crumpled envelope and extracted it. The door between the two offices stood open.

Last night she had composed and revised a dozen versions. Resigning via a letter was cowardly. Jonathan deserved to hear her decision directly. But she couldn't do it. She was afraid he would try to change her mind.

Her hands were sweating. Once she did this, there would be no going back. Just as she was ready to approach his desk and place her missive in a prominent position, a deep male voice came from behind her.

"Lisette. What are you doing?"

Rattled and breathless, she spun around, managing to stash the envelope in her skirt pocket. "Jonathan. You startled me. I thought you weren't home."

He cocked his head, giving her a quizzical smile. "I live here," he reminded her.

"Of course you do." She wiped her hands on her hips. "When you weren't at the office, I thought I might come out to the house. You know. In case you needed me." The lie rolled off her lips.

Jonathan barely seemed to register her awkward phrasing. For the first time she saw that his face was pale. And he seemed tense. Distracted.

"Jonathan? Is something wrong?" He couldn't have known what she was about to do...could he?

He stared at her. "It hasn't been a great day."

"I'm sorry. Is there anything I can do to help?" Maybe fate had saved her from really bad timing. This was not the look of a man who would take her resignation with equanimity.

"I don't know." He spoke the words slowly, almost as if he were in a daze.

Now his demeanor began to worry her. The Jonathan she knew was sharp and decisive, a brilliant boss who ran his massive company with an iron fist but was also scrupulously fair.

She touched his forearm briefly, mostly because she couldn't help herself. "What's going on? Did we lose the Porter deal?"

He shook his head. "No." He shuffled a few papers on his desk. "I sent you some emails last night. Why don't you handle those? Then I might dictate a few letters." He winced and put a hand to his head, his pallor deepening.

Lisette knew about the headaches. She and Jonathan worked together closely, and she was well aware that he had been plagued by the pain for months now.

"Have you taken anything?" she asked quietly. "I can see that you're hurting."

His grimace spoke volumes. "Yes. But not long ago."

"Why don't you go upstairs and lie down? You can forward your cell to the phone here. I'll come get you if it's anything urgent."

Even hurting and not at his best, Jonathan Tarleton was handsome and charismatic. He carried an aura of absolute control. Seeing him so vulnerable was both shocking and unsettling.

"An hour," he said gruffly. "No more. I'll set the alarm on my phone."

Jonathan climbed the stairs slowly. Reality began to sink in. This situation wasn't going to improve. He could get another opinion, but what was the use? He'd been to multiple doctors. This last set of tests was the first time he had received a definitive answer.

In his large, well-appointed bedroom, he cursed beneath his breath and admitted to himself that he needed the pills. He had to think clearly, and right now his head felt like someone was using it for a bongo drum.

Once he was sprawled on his comfortable mattress, he lay very still and waited for the meds to work. Knowing that Lisette was downstairs helped. Though he didn't doze, he let his mind wander. Slowly his body relaxed. Stress was a killer. The irony of that didn't escape him.

Thinking about Lisette was both comforting and arousing. She had been a part of his life for a long time now. His personal, rigid code of ethics meant that he never acted on his attraction to her. They were work colleagues. Nothing more. He had regretted that at times, but now he should be glad. He was going to need some-one in his corner who could be objective about what was to come.

Lisette was a soothing personality. Her competence and complete ability to handle any and every crisis were what had won him over in the beginning. He trusted her with any number of confidential work details, every-thing from high-level negotiations to financial secrets.

Some men might overlook her. Her brown hair and quiet personality were unremarkable. She had a femi-nine shape, but she didn't dress to impress. Her sexiest trait was her brain. She challenged him, kept him on his toes. The truth was, she was as capable as he, though she was always careful not to overstep her position.

Jonathan wouldn't have cared even if she had. He knew she could go to any company in the country or even abroad and land a prestigious job. For that reason, he had increased her salary in regular bumps to show her how much she was appreciated. And he had given her more and more responsibilities as she proved her loyalty to Tarleton Shipping.

Gradually the tension in his muscles began to ease. The pain in his head subsided to a dull ache instead of stabbing torture. As he began to feel more like himself, an idea bubbled to the surface.

What if he negotiated with Lisette to sub for him over the next few months when he wasn't able to function? He never knew from one day to the next how he was going to feel. If Lisette was deputized to make unilat-eral decisions, Jonathan would be able to mentally relax.

Better still, what if she could be the one to save Tar-leton Shipping for the next generation? She had the brains and the people skills. And he knew she cared deeply about the company.

It would also mean he could postpone telling his family for a little bit longer. The prospect of hurting the people he loved flayed him. How could he dump that kind of news on them? It might kill his father. Mazie and J.B. were struggling with fertility. They sure as hell didn't need grief on top of that.

The doctor had said he *might* have longer than six months. Eating well and getting plenty of rest were supposed to be key. Jonathan was willing to fight, but the odds were definitely not in his favor. If a cure was out of the question, then all he could hope for was time enough to secure his legacy and the company's future. The more he contemplated the next few months, the more he became convinced that Lisette was the key to it all.

At last he stood and raked his hands through his hair. After splashing water on his face, he studied his reflection in the mirror. He'd taken some hard knocks in his life, but this was the worst. Grimly he weighed the cost of bringing Lisette in on the secret. He couldn't stand to be pitied or coddled.

There would have to be ground rules. And she had to know this new role was optional. If she said no, he would go it alone.

By the time he padded back downstairs in his stocking feet, almost two hours had passed. Both offices were empty. He found Lisette perched on an ottoman chatting with his father. She always went out of her way to make the old man feel special.

Gerald Tarleton had become a father late in life. Which was why Jonathan, at thirty-one, now bore the sole responsibility for running a mammoth enterprise.

He strode into the room, watching both of their faces. Lisette's was serene. His father tried to give him a hard time.

"Napping in the middle of the day, son? That's my job."

Jonathan ruffled his father's hair and perched on the arm of the sofa. "I had a devil of a headache, but I'm feeling better now."

"Are you really?" Lisette asked, her gaze troubled.

He nodded. "Really." After a moment of chitchat about the weather, Jonathan stood. "You'll have to excuse us, Dad. Lisette and I have a few things to wrap up before she goes home."

"Of course. Besides, I've got to make sure the housekeeper has all the food ready. The boys are coming over for poker at six."

The "boys" were all Gerald's age. Jonathan was happy to see his father pursuing social interests. Both Mazie and Jonathan had been encouraging him to get out of the house more. He'd been depressed over the winter, but things were improving.

Lisette followed Jonathan back to the offices. "I took care of everything you sent me so far. Is there anything else you need today? If not, I'll see you downtown in the morning."

Jonathan stared at her intently, allowing his customary reserve to dissolve for a moment. Lisette was everything he liked in a woman and more. Beautiful, insightful, funny. And subtly sexy in a way some men might miss. Was he hatching this plan to save his family's business, or was his libido steering the ship?

He was about to find out.

Two

Jonathan knew this was an opening he couldn't pass up. But he had no idea how Lisette would react. He'd never felt uncomfortable around her before today. Then again, he'd never faced the prospect of shifting their relationship to a different footing.

She was the one person outside his small family circle whom he trusted completely. Not only with his secrets but with the future of his company and his personal legacy.

In order for such a fledgling plan to work, Lisette would have to be personally invested in what he was about to propose. She would have to be confident in her power and autonomy.

His burgeoning idea was a lot to dump on a woman. He would have to ease into it.

Maybe this was a stupid idea.

Lisette eyed him with curiosity in her gaze. Perhaps he wasn't as stoic as he had hoped. Or as guarded.

"I need to speak to you," he said carefully. "But not here. And it's not about work. Or at least not entirely."

Now her curiosity turned to confusion. "I don't understand."

Jonathan felt his neck heat. "If you would feel more comfortable, I could ask someone from HR to sit in on this conversation."

Her eyes widened. "Are you firing me?"

He gaped. "God, no. Are you insane? Why would I fire the best employee I've ever had?"

"Then what is this about?"

Jonathan swallowed. "Will you come to dinner with me?" he asked quietly. "We'll drive up the coast. Where we won't be seen. The matter I want to discuss with you is sensitive. I don't want to take advantage of your kindness, though, so feel free to say no."

Lisette shook her head slowly, her expression wry. "I've known you for a very long time, Jonathan. Dinner is fine. And we don't need a chaperone. Clearly, whatever you have to say is important. I'm happy to listen."

"Thank you."

She glanced down at her khaki skirt and sleeveless top. "Is what I'm wearing okay?"

He nodded slowly. "We might even take a picnic instead of going to a restaurant." There would be more privacy that way. No chance of anyone overhearing the conversation.

Though Lisette was clearly flustered, she didn't quibble over the plan. "I'm ready whenever you are. Do I need to drive?" she asked. "Because of the meds you took?"

"No. Not this time. I would never do anything to endanger you."

After quick goodbyes to Gerald, they exited the house. Jonathan tossed a couple of beach chairs into the back of the SUV. Being in the car together was definitely awkward. Her body language said she was uncertain of his intentions.

It didn't help that he was not big on small talk.

As he drove up the coast, he formulated a plan. Thirty minutes later, he pulled into a small fishing town and parked near a shed adjacent to the pier. This particular spot was more popular with locals than tourists. They ordered two shrimp baskets with large lemonades and took it to go.

Lisette teased him. "I pegged you as more of a beer than lemonade guy."

He shrugged. "Can't drink with the headache meds."

She winced. "Ah. Of course. Sorry."

Jonathan remembered a stretch of beach that was not particularly crowded. And this was the time of day that families headed inside to shower and clean up for dinner. As he suspected, there was plenty of open sand to be alone.

He carried the chairs. Lisette brought the food and drinks. The tide was headed out, so they picked a spot near a tidal pool and set up camp.

A light breeze blew in from the water. The sea was gunmetal gray, the sky streaked with golds and pinks, though sunset was a couple of hours away. Neither of them spoke as they opened their bags of food.

Jonathan sat back with a sigh. He'd lived near Charleston his entire life. The water was a part of him.

The sand. The steady inexorable pull of the tides. Why did he spend so much time inside working?

It was human nature, he supposed, to take things for granted. After all, the sea would always be there. What had never occurred to him was that *he* wouldn't. He was measuring his life in months now, not years. Soon the parameters would be smaller than that. Weeks. Days.

Choking anger swelled in his chest. He didn't want to die. It wasn't fair. He felt as if he had only begun to live. But if he had to go, he wanted Lisette to protect his reputation and everything he had worked so hard to build.

Beside him, she ate her meal in silence, her gaze trained on the horizon. What was she thinking?

He had to speak his piece. But how? Even now, the words seemed ridiculous. Overly dramatic. *By the way, I'm living on borrowed time. Thought you should know.*

Part of him wanted to take off running down the beach and never stop. Perhaps if he ran fast enough and far enough, the grim reaper couldn't keep up. Perhaps this was all a bad dream.

Lisette leaned forward and set her cup in the sand, twisting it until it stayed upright. She tucked her trash in the bag and sat back, eyes closed. "That was lovely," she said. "I should have dinner at the beach every day."

"Not a bad idea."

The silence built between them, but it wasn't unpleasant. The ocean lulled their senses, washing away the stresses of the day.

Lisette reached out one leg and dabbled the tip of her sandal in the tidal pool, not looking at him. "So what's this big secret? Talk to me, Jonathan."

His stomach clenched. His jaw tightened. "I have a brain tumor," he said flatly. "Inoperable. Terminal."

* * *

Icy disbelief swept over her body and through her veins as if she'd been doused with winter rain and left to shiver and convulse in a stark landscape. No. It couldn't be true.

Slowly she turned to face him. Her shaking hands twisted in her lap. "Are you positive?" It was a stupid question. No one tossed around statements like that unless they were sure.

His bleak profile matched his body language as he stared at the water. "Oh, yeah." His low laugh held no humor. "The latest test results came in this morning."

"I'm so sorry," she whispered.

"I don't know how long I have," he said. "And I don't know what to expect. Which is why I'm having this conversation with you. I don't want to tell my family yet. I thought you could be an impartial…"

He trailed off, clearly searching for a word.

"A friend? A colleague?" The impossibility of what he was asking staggered her.

"You're more than that," he said huskily. "I trust you implicitly. I want to give you the authority to step in and make decisions if I'm having a bad day. I realize this is asking a lot of you, but I'll change your title and compensate you accordingly."

"Shouldn't Hartley be the one to fill this role?" She had never quite understood why he disappeared.

Jonathan's expression turned glacial. "My brother is gone and he's not coming back. It's not something I can discuss with you."

"But surely your other family members need to know. You can't keep this a secret, Jonathan."

"I realize that." His fists were clenched on the arms

of the chair. "But I have to find the right time. I'll wait as long as I can."

She wanted to argue with him. For everyone's sake. But once Jonathan Tarleton made up his mind, you'd have better luck moving a giant boulder than changing his decision.

The enormity of what he had told her began to sink in. Her heart was raw and broken. She loved him. That's why she had planned to leave. How could she stay with him day after day and witness the unthinkable? It would destroy her. But how could she say no when he needed her?

"I'd like to think about it overnight," she said. "I'm not sure I feel comfortable trying to insert myself into company politics. There are a lot of people who won't take kindly to this setup."

"I'm the boss. What I say goes."

"But what about the board of directors? And your father, Gerald? And what happens when you become too ill to work?"

Her throat tightened with tears, tears she couldn't shed. He thought she was an impartial bystander. How much more wrong could he be?

"I need to walk," she said.

"Okay." Jonathan stood as well, shrugging out of his sport coat and rolling up the sleeves of his crisp cotton dress shirt.

They took off their shoes and headed down the beach. Jonathan matched his long stride to her shorter one, because he topped her by six inches. His chestnut hair was burnished by the setting sun. The dark brown eyes, which could be fierce or good-humored, were hidden behind sunglasses.

His arms were deeply tanned, his hands masculine.

He was a beautiful human being. It was almost impossible to imagine that vitality and charisma being snuffed out.

At last, after half an hour passed, the tension dissipated and re-formed into something else. Awareness.

At least on her part. Being with him like this was a physical pain. When had she first realized he was the one? Long before she became his assistant. The fact that he was completely out of her orbit had kept her crush in check. But working together day after day had turned her fluttery feelings into something far deeper and more real.

She not only loved him, she admired and respected him. In a world where men in power sometimes abused their positions, Jonathan Tarleton had never treated his employees, female *or* male, with careless disregard.

If he had any faults at all, and he surely did, the most visible was his careful aloofness. He kept to himself, never blurring the lines between his authority and those who worked for him.

That fact made today's revelations all the more stunning.

They were walking shoulder to shoulder, so close she could have reached out and touched his hand. The beach was almost deserted now, the daylight fading rapidly as the sun kissed the water at the horizon.

Taking a deep breath, she halted and waited for him to follow suit.

He turned when he realized she had dropped back. "Time to go home?" he asked lightly.

"I'll do it," she said recklessly. "I'll do what you asked."

"I thought you needed to think it over."

She shook her head. "You and your family have been very good to me. It's only right that I should return the favor."

Jonathan removed his sunglasses and tucked them into his shirt pocket. "We sent flowers and gave you time off when your mother passed." He frowned. "It's not the same thing at all. What I'm asking you to do is nebulous and tricky and burdensome."

Burdensome. The word made her want to laugh, but not in a good way. Walking beside Jonathan for the next weeks and months would tax her emotional strength and her acting ability.

"I'm honored," she said slowly, trying not to give her secrets away. "I care about you, Jonathan. You're facing some very dark days. So, yes, I'll help you any way I can."

She saw his chest rise and fall. Had he been so uncertain that she would agree to his proposal?

His throat rippled as he swallowed. His gaze held a bleak acknowledgment of what he faced. "Thank you."

The two words were little more than a croak.

Tears stung her eyes. Without overthinking it, she went up on her tiptoes and kissed his cheek. Then she wrapped her arms around his stiff body in a brief hug. "I'm so very sorry," she said.

He might as well have been a statue. "I have rules," he said gruffly.

"Oh?" She shoved the hair from her face. Standing with the wind at her back made her feel disheveled.

"I won't be coddled." He snapped the words. "And I don't want your pity. Understood?"

She recoiled inwardly, but she kept her expression

calm. "I can live with that. But when I see that you need help, I'll give it. So that's my rule, I suppose. I won't stand by and let you suffer if I can do anything about it."

He blinked. Apparently the kiss and the hug hadn't shocked him as much as her talking back to him with belligerence in her voice.

A tiny smile tilted the corners of his mouth. "I've spent most of the day thinking I'd never have anything to laugh about again. You just proved me wrong. Have I had a lioness in my midst disguised as a kitty cat all this time?"

Her face heated. "Things are about to change between us," she said quietly. "Are you sure this is what you want?"

He leaned forward and brushed his lips against her cheek, barely a touch at all. "I am. I do."

Something made her legs go all wonky. For a moment, she thought she might faint. If that was how a kiss from Jonathan affected her when he was being amused and affectionate, God help her if she ever experienced the real thing. She tried to suck in more air. "Okay then."

Jonathan looped his arm through hers and turned them around. "It's late," he said. "We need to get you home."

She would have slept in her car on the street if it had meant not ending this extraordinary interlude. His skin was warm against hers. She wanted to lean her head against his shoulder, but of course, she did not.

Something had happened here on this beach. The tides in her relationship with her boss had shifted to something far more real, more intimate. Unfortunately, she couldn't even be glad about that change, because it meant she was losing him.

Back at the car, they dusted off their feet and used a water bottle for their impromptu cleanup. When Jonathan started the engine, he glanced sideways at her. "Dessert and coffee before we head back?"

Yes, her heart cried. Yes!

She shook her head. "It's been a long day. I'd better not."

"Of course." He paused. "I think it goes without saying, but you must promise not to talk to anyone about my condition. *No one.* If the truth were to come out, our stock prices might plummet. Until I have a plan in place to handle the gossip and the fallout, there can't be a whisper that anything is wrong."

"I understand. You have my word."

They barely spoke during the drive back. Without the beauty of the ocean and the beach to distract them, the enormity of Jonathan's diagnosis filled her with aching compassion and raw regret. How could this be happening? It wasn't fair. Not for him, not for his family, not for anyone.

But whoever said life was fair?

When they reached the Tarleton house, she exited the vehicle and stood beside her own car. In the unflattering glow of the security light beneath the house, Jonathan's expression was grim, his skin sallow.

He seemed so damned brave and alone. She couldn't leave him like this.

Rounding the car, she went to him and slid her arms around his waist. He wasn't her boss at this moment. He was a man nearing a perilous cliff, a human being with little more than sheer grit and determination to help him face the days ahead.

At first, he was unresponsive. Maybe her emotion

was only making things worse. Finally, a great shudder racked his frame. He buried his face in her hair and clung to her tightly.

Her tears wet his shirt. "I'm so sorry, Jonathan. So very sorry."

They stood there like that for long moments. It might have been a minute or five or ten.

At last he straightened. He used his thumb to catch a tear on her lower lashes. "Don't cry for me, Lizzy. I'd rather it be me than someone else. Hell, I probably deserve it."

She stepped back reluctantly and stared up at him. "Don't joke," she said. "There's nothing remotely funny about this situation."

His smile was both weary and beautiful. "Isn't that what they say? I have to laugh to keep from crying?"

"I can't imagine you crying. You're tough and resourceful. Very macho, in fact."

"Is that how you see me?"

She shrugged. "You've been my boss. I only looked at you one way."

"And now?"

Was this some kind of trick question?

She hesitated. "I know you're human, Jonathan. Just like the rest of us. But I never wanted to test that theory. I'd rather think of you as a superhero than admit the truth right now."

His wince echoed her honesty. "You and me both. This won't be easy for me. And I'm not talking about the physical part. The prospect of not being in control scares the hell out of me."

"I'll be here, Jonathan. But you *have* to tell your

family. They'll be so hurt if you don't and they find out another way."

He shoved his hands into his pockets. "I'll tell them. I swear. I just need a little time to wrap my head around this."

"Have you thought about seeing a counselor or a priest…someone like that? It might help."

He cupped her cheek in one big palm, his touch burning her skin and sending shivers of sensation in every direction. "I have you, Lisette. That will have to do."

Three

Lisette cried herself to sleep. And then had nightmares. Waking at dawn was a relief for half a second until the truth came rushing back with a vengeance. Jonathan was dying.

Thank God, she hadn't turned in her resignation before he told her about his illness. He needed her. She was determined to give him all the love and care she could muster…but without letting on that she had loved him for a long time. That news would make things worse. She knew it instinctively.

The only reason he had asked for her help was because she was an outsider he could trust. So—not family.

Walking into the downtown office that morning was anticlimactic. Jonathan was on a conference call with someone in England. The entire floor was abuzz with the usual ebb and flow of projects and activities.

Lisette loved working for Tarleton Shipping. As hard as it had been to make the decision to leave, it was impossible to imagine this place without Jonathan. She pressed a hand to her stomach where nervous butterflies performed a tango.

Last night at the beach house had changed everything.

Somehow, she was supposed to carry on as if nothing was out of the ordinary, but at the same time she had to monitor Jonathan's behavior and be ready to step in whenever he needed her. She wondered if he was regretting that he had told her the truth.

Yesterday had been an extraordinarily hard time for him. Hearing news like that would rattle anyone. The fact that Lisette had shown up at his house in the wake of his crisis might have had something to do with him asking her to take on a role that was so personal and critical.

If she knew him well—and she did—it was probably best to pretend nothing had changed. It was going to be very hard not to hover and treat him like he was sick. She couldn't help feeling responsible, especially because he was keeping his family in the dark for now.

The day spun by, entirely unremarkable in its *ordinariness*. People came and went. Meetings happened. Jonathan whirled from one thing to the next, barely speaking to her in the interim.

She could almost believe that last night was a dream.

Occasionally, though, she caught his eye across the room, and a connection quivered between them. The feeling of intimacy startled her. He had let her in on something intensely personal. There would be no going back from this.

She had craved a personal connection with Jonathan. But not at this price.

How was she going to face the days ahead?

On her lunch hour, her friend Rebekah coaxed her out of the building. "Let's walk," she said. "It's not quite so hot today, and I've been wanting to try that new restaurant over near the market."

There was nothing unusual about the situation. Still, Lisette felt Jonathan's gaze searing her back as she exited the executive suite of offices. Did he expect her to dance attendance on him 24/7?

Rebekah called her out on her odd mood while they ate. "What's wrong with you?" she asked, frowning. "You've barely said a word. Are you feeling okay?"

"I'm fine," Lisette said. "A lot on my mind."

Her friend's expression softened. "I just realized. Today marks eight months since your mother died, doesn't it? I'm sorry, hon."

Guilt swamped Lisette. Her friend had metaphorically and literally held her hand during some very dark days. "I'm getting used to her being gone. I find new reasons to be happy every day. My mother wouldn't have wanted me to be gloomy all the time."

"Well, good," Rebekah said. "Because Robbie's friend who just moved here from Memphis wants to meet you. I thought we could go to dinner together Friday night."

Lisette winced inwardly. Rebekah had been on her case for months to start dating. Caring for her mother and working full-time had not left any room for a social life. Now that her mother was gone and months had passed, it made sense for Lisette to get back in the game.

She was torn. The trouble was, she didn't want to

meet a string of strange guys, even though she knew her dream of marriage and a baby required some kind of change on her part. She didn't need clubbing and dancing to be happy. The only man she wanted was Jonathan. Their new situation would give her a little piece of him. Would it be enough to justify putting her dreams on hold?

"Sure," she said, trying hard to appreciate her friend's enthusiasm. "That sounds great."

The following two days passed in much the same manner, at least when it came to Jonathan's behavior. He didn't *look* sick. Aside from downing the occasional over-the-counter meds, his bronzed skin and boundless energy seemed to belie his diagnosis.

When Friday afternoon rolled around, Lisette was almost glad Jonathan was away from the office. Their new relationship made her both tense and uncertain. It was a relief to step out into the sunshine and walk to her car. She had just enough time to dash home, shower and change before she met Rebekah and the others at the restaurant.

It was a shock to run into her boss in the parking garage. He looked frazzled, but otherwise normal. "You're leaving?" he asked.

She nodded her head. "It's five thirty. Was there something you needed?"

His small frown took her by surprise. "I thought we might have dinner together," he said. "To talk about how we're going to handle this new work situation."

She flushed, feeling the heat creep from her breasts to her hairline. "I'm sorry," she said stiffly. "I have plans."

He seemed shocked. "A date?"

"That's a personal question," she snapped. His obvious surprise nicked her pride. It was true she had lived like a nun while caring for her mother. And, yes, she was five years Jonathan's senior. But she was hardly a pariah.

His gaze darkened. "I'm sorry to have held you up," he said, his tone stiff and formal. "I'll see you Monday morning."

The bleak expression in his eyes caught her heart and squeezed it hard. She was trying so desperately to protect herself, to avoid letting him hurt her, that she was forgetting the hell he was facing.

"Wait," she said impulsively as he turned to walk away. "What about lunch at my place Sunday? I'll cook for you."

Some of the starch left his spine. At last a smile tilted those gorgeous masculine lips. "That sounds great, Lisette. If you're sure it's not too much trouble."

"Not at all. And by the way, I've moved since my mother died. I'm in a condo in North Charleston now." Her salary was generous, but it didn't stretch to upscale places in the historic district.

He nodded. "I'll get the address from your file."

"Noon?"

"I'll be there."

The unexpected encounter meant she had to rush like crazy to go home and then meet her friend. She made it to the restaurant with two minutes to spare. Her blind date for the evening was overly chatty, but all in all a decent guy. Under other circumstances, she might have hoped for a second date.

As it was, though, she found her mind wandering

time and again during the pleasant meal to Jonathan. What was he doing? How was he feeling?

When the two females left the table to visit the ladies' room, Rebekah leaned in to whisper conspiratorially. "Well, what do you think of him? He likes you. I can tell."

Lisette made use of the facilities and then washed her hands. "I don't know, Rebekah. He isn't really my type."

Rebekah snorted. "You don't *have* a type," she said. "This is the first time I've coaxed you out of the house. At least give him a chance. It's not like you've got your heart set on someone else."

"I'll keep an open mind, I swear."

Lisette had been careful at work to hide her feelings about Jonathan, from Rebekah in particular. She'd kept her hopeless crush a secret from everyone. When Lisette had been planning to resign, she was going to tell her friend that she was in a rut after her mother's death and that she needed a fresh start. Now those heavy-handed explanations weren't going to be necessary.

But there would be other questions when she began spending more time with Jonathan. She would have to spin the story somehow to protect his secret. And if her so-called promotion became public knowledge, the situation would definitely become awkward.

At last the interminable evening wound to a close. She had never been more glad to head home and crash. Even then, she couldn't stop thinking about her boss. He had chosen to confide his secret in her. She couldn't pretend any longer that she didn't want to be much more than his stand-in at work.

He was ferociously smart and driven. The man *did* have a sense of humor, but it was dry and often kept under wraps. Because his father had been forced to step down as president when his health deteriorated, Jonathan bore a heavy load of responsibility.

All day Saturday Lisette obsessed about what to cook, what to wear. She was terrified of letting her boss know that her emotions were involved. If she was going to be able to help, she had to let him think she regarded this as a job and nothing more.

By Sunday morning, she had worked herself into a full-blown tizzy. When her curling iron failed to do what she wanted it to do, she gave up styling her thick, straight hair and put it up in a ponytail.

She didn't want to look like she thought this was a date, so she put on an older pair of jeans, black ballerina flats and a cute teal top with a lemon print. A dash of lip gloss and some mascara took care of the rest.

By the time her tomato sauce was ready and the simple fruit salad cut and arranged in crystal bowls, she felt mildly nauseous. What was she thinking? She should have resigned as she had planned.

She was weak when it came to her boss. This was a chance to be with him in a way she wouldn't otherwise. It "was" an intimacy of sorts. A dangerous intimacy she both yearned for and feared.

Instead of getting *over* Jonathan, she was only going to fall more deeply under his spell and end up having her heart broken into a million unmendable pieces. Broken because he couldn't love her back, and broken because soon he would be gone from her life forever.

Her buzzer rang at exactly eleven fifty-nine. That was *so* Jonathan. The man made punctuality a religion.

She opened the door and managed a smile. "Good

morning, or I guess it's officially afternoon now. Come on in."

Her knees wobbled when the scent of his crisp after-shave teased her nostrils. His broad shoulders were encased in a simple white cotton shirt. Rolled-up sleeves revealed muscular arms tanned from years in the sun. An expensive watch gleamed on one wrist.

He was dressed more casually than she had ever seen him. Jeans, too, like her. Leather deck shoes that drew attention to his sexy feet.

When she realized she was getting turned on by the man's feet, she knew she was in big trouble.

Her big, sexy guest smiled. "Smells amazing in here."

Jonathan was gobsmacked and trying not to show it. What had happened to the prim and proper woman who managed his business affairs with such aplomb? Suddenly…today…she looked barely twenty. Her smooth, creamy skin was unadorned. That perky ponytail bared the nape of her neck.

Her lightweight summer blouse fit her generous breasts snugly. And those skinny jeans? Hell. A man could be excused for wanting to cup that heart-shaped butt in his two hands. His libido, which in recent days had been squashed, roared back to life in a big way.

Was his reaction inappropriate? Should he try harder to ignore the attraction? Or, under the circumstances, could he be excused for wanting to let himself finally get closer to Lisette?

He shifted from one foot to the other. "This is very nice of you," he said. "I've been looking forward to a home-cooked meal."

Lisette gave him a look, one eyebrow raised. "You

have the best housekeeper and chef in the state of South Carolina."

"It's not the same as having a woman cook for me."

He hadn't intended to bring flirtation into the mix, not at all. But the comment slipped out.

Far from being offended, Lisette gave him a shy smile. "Sit down at the table," she said. "Everything is almost ready."

He sprawled in a trendy retro chair that reminded him of something his great-grandmother might have used back in the 1950s. The Formica-top table was aqua and white. In the center sat a white hobnail vase filled with daisies. Yellow place mats had been set with flatware and cloth napkins.

"I like your condo," he said.

"Thanks. I needed a change of scenery after Mom died. This building is very friendly, and I like the neighborhood."

"Does the guy you were out with Friday night live here?" The question popped out of his mouth before he could censor it. Entirely inappropriate from boss to employee. Entirely understandable from a man who felt like he was losing everything. His whole life had shifted. Inappropriate feelings he had suppressed for so long in the past were coming to the fore.

Lisette had her back to him, grating fresh parmesan cheese for their spaghetti. He saw her go still. But she didn't turn around. "No," she said quietly. "That was a blind date my friend Rebekah set up."

"Rebekah in Purchasing?"

"Yes."

He drummed his fingers on the table. "Sorry," he muttered. "None of my business."

She turned to face him with an unreadable expression on her face. "This is not going to work unless we can both speak freely. Under the circumstances, I understand that you want to know more about my life. If I'm going to help you, you have to trust me."

"I *do* trust you," he said quickly. "Completely."

"But?" Her half smile called him out.

Clearly she was reading his ambivalence. "I think you were right about the possibility of people resenting you if I suddenly give you carte blanche to make decisions."

She nodded slowly. "It *will* look odd. Does this mean you've changed your mind?"

He stood to pace restlessly, shoving his hands in his pockets. Second-guessing himself was a novelty he didn't enjoy. In almost any situation he was able to cut through to the center of a matter and make decisions… good decisions. But that was business.

This new scenario with Lisette comprised a hundred more layers of uncertainty. "I haven't changed my mind," he said. "But I've had more time to think about this, and I've come to a few conclusions."

"Sounds important," she said lightly, pouring each of them a glass of iced tea.

"It will keep until after we've eaten. I always think better on a full stomach. And have your wine," he said. "You don't have to abstain on my account."

She shook her head. "I happen to love iced tea. Mine is very good, if I do say so myself. My grandmother taught my mom, and my mom taught me."

"I know very little about your family," he said.

"Not much to tell." Lisette set white porcelain salad bowls, dressing, and the two plates of steaming pasta on the table, along with a smaller plate of fragrant garlic bread. Jonathan held out her chair as she seated herself. Then he took the spot opposite her.

"Is your father still living?" he asked. "I don't remember hearing you say."

She shook her head. "My mother never spoke of him. As a kid I fantasized that he was a secret agent or a prince in some foreign country. Unfortunately, I think the truth is that he just didn't care and walked away."

"Were they married?"

"I believe so. There's a name on my birth certificate. And it's the same last name as my mom's and mine. But she could have made him up."

"Haven't you ever wanted to track him down?"

Lisette grimaced, a bite of spaghetti halfway to her mouth. She set the fork on her plate and sighed. "According to all the books and movies, I should. Want to, I mean. But the truth is, I don't."

"Why not?" Jonathan had cleared most of his plate. He was starving, and the meal was amazing. Lisette had barely picked at her spaghetti. Was it because she was nervous? He hoped not. He wanted things between them to be comfortable. Easy.

Maybe that was an impossible task under the circumstances.

She curled her fingers around the stem of her crystal goblet and wrinkled her nose. "My mom did the best she could for us, but I was a latchkey kid from the time I was eight or nine. Our house wasn't like my friends' houses. It was quiet and empty and lonely. I decided that I would make my own home someday and fill it with color and sound and happiness."

Jonathan nodded and smiled. "You're off to a good

start." Inwardly he groaned. His needs and wants were going to be in direct opposition to hers. Was it fair of him to ask so much when he could give her so little in return?

"Thank you." Her cheeks were flushed. It could be the heat from the kitchen, or perhaps she was as aware of him as he was of her. Before today, he would have said that he knew Lisette Stanhope extremely well. Now, here in her cozy, peaceful home, he was finding out how wrong he could be.

Away from the office, she seemed a different person to him. Younger, more vulnerable. Again his conscience pricked him. Lisette was conscientious and compassionate. Last year when one of their employees suffered an extended illness, Lisette was the one who organized meals for the family.

She had been a devoted daughter and caretaker to her mother for a decade or more. Jonathan didn't want to be another burden she had to carry. To be honest, he didn't want to be *anyone's* burden, but especially not hers.

If they were to enter into this arrangement, the benefits couldn't and shouldn't be one-sided. It was becoming more and more clear to him that there was only one real way for this new relationship to work. A drastic step that would change everything.

As the silence between them lengthened, Lisette finished most of her meal. Jonathan had a second helping of everything.

"Thank you for cooking," he said. Something about the simple, hearty meal fed his soul as well as his stomach. Food was one of a man's appetites. Sexual intimacy was another. The fact that he felt jittery and hungry for his hostess was as much a shock to him as what he was about to say.

They cleared the table together. Lisette started the dishwasher, and then she touched him lightly on the shoulder. "Let's go into the living room. We'll be more comfortable."

The few steps between the two rooms did not give him time enough to prepare a speech.

Lisette kicked off her shoes and settled onto one end of the sofa, her legs curled beneath her. "Well," she said. "Don't keep me in suspense. If I'm not to have a promotion, what's your answer?"

He sucked in a breath, feeling more rattled and off his game than he had since the day of his diagnosis. "I think you should marry me."

Four

Lisette blinked, trying not to react. "Um…" Maybe the brain tumor had begun to affect his reasoning. Or maybe she had misheard him.

Jonathan witnessed her shock despite her efforts to play it cool. His neck heated beneath his collar. "I'm not crazy," he muttered. "But it would solve a lot of problems. No one at the office would complain if I make my *wife* my partner. We could work side by side. This is the Tarleton empire. For you to pull off the kinds of decisions you'll be required to make, you need to be family. It's the perfect solution."

Except it wasn't. The mere fact that her emotions went all gooey at the prospect meant she would be seriously crazy to accept such an offer. She wanted him. She wanted to be married, but not like this.

When she had attempted to turn in her resignation

last week, she had been imagining a future with an ordinary guy. Maybe a teacher…or an accountant like herself. Two babies. Perhaps three. A small house with toys in the yard and even the proverbial picket fence. Everything she had missed growing up when it was only a single mom and a lonely daughter.

Now fate, or a deity with a messed-up sense of humor, was offering her a skewed version of that dream. "I don't know what to say." It was true. Jonathan had left her speechless.

He sprawled in an armchair, looking masculine and gorgeous and moody. "Say you'll think about it."

She chose her words carefully. "It seems like an extreme measure."

"But you have to admit it's a practical solution."

"Where would we live?"

"Out at the beach house."

"But I just bought this place, and I love it."

"You could sublet it. Or leave it empty and come here when you need a break from…" He waved a hand. "I'll pay for whatever you need. Money won't be a problem. We'll have a prenup that outlines everything you're entitled to when I'm gone."

He was talking about his illness. Addressing the elephant in the room. She didn't want to think about that.

Other issues weighed as heavily. "I'll be hated and vilified," she said. "When the truth comes out. Your family and your friends and your employees will think I deliberately married a dying man to get my hands on a chunk of Tarleton Shipping."

"It doesn't matter what anyone else thinks," he said, his tone truculent. "Our private arrangement is no one else's business. Dad won't question anything, and Mazie isn't going to squawk. She has plenty of her own assets, not to mention the fact that she married J.B."

Jonathan's best friend and his sister had gotten engaged last Christmas. Everyone assumed the two of them would plan a huge Charleston wedding, but the couple had surprised everyone by jetting off to Vegas in the middle of January and tying the knot in a private ceremony. The groom's mother had thrown the party of all parties when they returned.

Lisette had been invited and had attended despite the fact that she hadn't been in a celebratory mood. The gray days of January had exacerbated her grief. The new year had stretched ahead of her, long and lonely.

In the end, the party had done her good. It was fun, for one thing. It had warmed her heart to see Jonathan's sister so happy and in love with her rakish husband. *J.B.* as he was called, Jackson Beauregard Vaughan, was a real estate tycoon. He and the Tarletons had been friends since they were all children. Only Hartley Tarleton had been missing from the festivities.

Jonathan, himself, had been resplendent that night in a conservative tailored tux. He'd had women flocking around him like so many chattering mynah birds. That had been Lisette's first inkling that she was going to have to either get over her desperate crush somehow or move entirely out of his orbit and find herself a new life.

Now he stared at her so intently her nipples beaded beneath her top. She crossed her arms over her chest. "You can't just toss this at me and expect an instant answer."

His smile was unexpectedly sweet. "I know you, Lizzy. You're a lot like me. Pragmatic. Decisive. You don't dither. I've always admired that about you."

"Flattery will get you nowhere."

He chuckled. "Admit it. My plan makes perfect sense."

Lisette chewed the inside of her lip, far more tempted than she should have been. He hadn't mentioned marriage between them in any context but work. Yet there were a lot of hours in the day when the two of them *wouldn't* be working. How did he foresee that part of their relationship unfolding?

Was this to be a marriage of convenience? A paper commitment that she would look after him and have his back when he asked for assistance? She didn't require a sham marriage to do that. Jonathan was in a very bad situation, and he needed her help. She would give it gladly.

"There must be another way," she said.

"Why make it more difficult than it has to be? I'm asking a hell of a lot, I realize. And to be honest, it will soothe my conscience to know that you'll have financial security when I'm gone. It's the very least I can do considering what you're offering me in return."

"I don't want your money, Jonathan."

"Maybe not, but that's my condition. Life won't be easy for whoever takes over Tarleton Shipping. It will either have to be you or Mazie, and I'm almost a hundred percent certain she doesn't want that responsibility."

"Neither do I," Lisette protested. "I'll help you all I can in the short term. Because we're friends and you're a decent human being who is in a terrible spot. But I won't profit from simply doing the right thing."

"So what happens to the business when I'm no longer able to look after things?"

"I don't know, Jonathan. I really don't. Maybe we both need to give this some thought before we make any irrevocable decisions."

"I'd like to work on the legal documents soon." A bleak look flashed across his face. "The uncertainty of my condition compels me to get things nailed down as quickly as possible."

"How long do I have to decide?"

He shrugged. "Forty-eight hours?"

It wasn't much time. She inhaled, her fingers digging into the arm of the sofa. "And what about the physical side of our relationship?"

For the barest of moments, his jaw dropped. Perhaps her candor had shocked him. But he recovered quickly. His gaze was calm though his eyes flashed hot. "That will, of course, be entirely up to you. I don't think it's the kind of question that should be addressed in a pre-nup. You're a very appealing woman. We'll be living together. Our arrangement can be platonic or physical. I won't ask anything of you that you aren't prepared to give."

The intimation was unmistakable. He would be *interested* in taking her to bed. Hearing such a thing destroyed Lisette's ability to think clearly. It had never occurred to her that she was the kind of woman to attract Jonathan's attention under *any* circumstances. To have him address the subject so matter-of-factly stunned her.

"Very well," she said slowly. "I agree to think about all this for forty-eight hours."

Jonathan's nod was terse. "I'll get my lawyer started on the nuts and bolts of the contract. You should be considering anything specific you want included in the document."

"Like what? Movie-star demands? Orange M&M's on my desk every morning? Water from the French Alps? A personal assistant?"

At last Jonathan ceased wearing a path in her rug and sat down at the opposite end of the sofa with a weary grin. "Very funny. But the details are important to me. If we go through with this, your whole life will change. Any personal dreams you have will need to be put on hold. It hardly seems fair, but I'm desperate enough to ask."

He was right. The truth was sobering. She would be giving him six months of her life or—if Jonathan were lucky—maybe a year.

All the reasons she had wanted to resign still existed. Jonathan was almost thirty-two years old. She was thirty-seven. Far too old for him under normal circumstances, at least by her reckoning. Over the long years of caring for her mother, Lisette had missed out on all sorts of coming-of-age experiences. The carefree vacations abroad. The fun and frivolity of a weekend social life. Casual dating. She didn't regret it. She would never regret the time she had spent with her mother. And she would do it again in a heartbeat.

When you loved someone, you gave whatever the situation demanded in order to make that person a priority. Jonathan had chosen her because he thought she could be objective. It was her task to prove him right. She would make the sacrifice gladly, but he could never know why. He could never know she loved him. That knowledge would only add to the burden he carried.

It seemed so damned unfair to become part of his

life and yet still never have him. Not completely. Her throat was thick with tears.

She sensed he needed assurance that she was taking him seriously. "Don't worry, Jonathan. I'll obsess about this day and night, and then I'll settle in for the long haul. I'm not flippant about the situation, honestly."

"Fair enough." He glanced at his watch. "I've got work to do, so I'd better head back to the beach."

"It's the weekend. Don't you think you need to rest?"

"I'll rest when I'm dead."

It was the kind of comedic one-liner workaholics used all the time, a way to describe and justify a manic schedule. Today Lisette found no humor in it.

She stood when he did, a good six feet of real estate between them.

Jonathan rolled his neck and shoved his hands into his pockets. "Thanks for the meal. It was fabulous."

Suddenly, she knew that she couldn't enter into this unconventional agreement without at least a few answers to questions that were…*sensitive*. She and Jonathan were going to be very close. Especially as the months passed and he leaned on her more and more.

She was tired of living like a nun…tired of denying she was a woman with needs and desires like everyone else. She wanted Jonathan, had wanted him for so very long. If his oblique remarks were revealing, he wanted her, too.

Before she could lose her nerve, she went to him and put her hands on his shoulders. Though she felt him tense, she continued her experiment.

"Will you kiss me, Jonathan?" she whispered, her throat tight. "I need to know if we have a spark, or if I'm only going to be your stand-in at work and possibly your nurse. I'm not making light of this. It's important to me."

His eyes could range from cognac to dark chocolate. Right now they were lit with a flame that took her breath and made her knees go weak. "As you wish," he said quietly.

Carefully he cupped her neck in two big hands and tilted her head slightly to one side. After that—as their breath mingled—he found her mouth and covered her lips with his. "Oh…" Her startled exclamation was involuntary. At first, the kiss was awkward and slightly embarrassing. He was her boss. She was his assistant. Before today, she would never have dreamed of crossing this line.

His kiss was firm and perfect, but her body was rigid, uncertain.

Jonathan made a sound low in his throat…a groan. A ragged sigh. "Relax, Lisette."

She tried, she really did. Her universe was cartwheeling out of control. He dragged her closer, deepening the kiss, pressing her to him in such a way that she couldn't miss the evidence of his body responding to hers. His sex rose and thrust against her abdomen.

Pulling back was the correct thing to do. Breaking the connection. Reclaiming sanity.

Neither of them chose to be wise.

Jonathan tugged the tie from her ponytail and sifted his fingers through the thickness of her shoulder-length hair. When his fingers brushed the nape of her neck, she shivered.

She was within seconds of pulling him down onto her sofa when her dormant sense of self-preservation shouted a warning. This wasn't a fairy tale. She was about to travel a road that ended in disaster.

Reluctantly she stepped back, breathing hard, trembling in every cell and trying not to show it. "Well," she said, trying for amused nonchalance. "I suppose we answered that question. If we decide to be friends with benefits, the spark is there."

Jonathan's frown was dark. With his hair disheveled where her hands had raked through it and his face flushed with the remnants of arousal, he looked dangerously disgruntled.

"It's not something to joke about. I won't be with other women if you're my wife. I'd expect the same courtesy from you."

She wanted to laugh. The thought of sleeping with another man while married to her boss was ludicrous. But Jonathan would probably misunderstand her reaction. So she pressed her lips together and tried to look penitent.

"Of course," she muttered. "One step at a time. First we have to decide if marriage would be convenient or impossibly convoluted."

He folded his arms and took a stance that was definitely more stubborn male than obsequious suitor. "There's nothing to decide. You know I'm right. It's the only way. Unless you've changed your mind about helping me."

She lifted her chin, matching him glare for glare. "I won't be bullied. I want to examine the pros and cons from every direction. You're correct in saying that I'm decisive as a rule. But I've never been an impulsive person. I don't plan to start now."

He would have been well within his rights to point

out that her recent behavior was damned impulsive. Fortunately for her, he held his tongue on that matter.

"Tuesday night," he said firmly. "My father is taking an overnight fishing trip with J.B.'s dad. They've been planning it for months. I'll have the housekeeper fix us a meal, and then we can walk the beach."

Lisette nodded slowly. "Okay. I like the sound of that. And just so we're clear, *you* can change your mind, too. I know the news of your diagnosis threw you into a tailspin. It would have knocked anyone on their butt. Give yourself more time to think this through. You won't hurt my feelings if you see another way out of your situation."

She didn't tell him that if he did, she would soon be gone.

Jonathan shook his head doggedly. "I've already come up with the perfect plan. Now it's simply a question of implementation."

"Very well."

He reached for his wallet and keys. "You'll be at work in the morning?"

She raised an eyebrow. "Of course. Where else would I be?"

Nodding tersely, he strode toward the door. "I'll see you then." It was a small condo. He was on the doorstep in moments.

"Wait," she cried.

He turned and stared at her. "What?"

"Jonathan..." She trailed off, not entirely sure how to say what she wanted to say.

"What?"

Impatience was painted all over his face. For a man who had seemed very happy to spend part of the afternoon with her, he was now clearly itching to leave. Maybe he had regrets, too.

"You don't seem all that sick," she said slowly, not wanting to anger him. "I know about the headaches, but what if the doctor was wrong?"

His jaw jutted and his hands fisted at his sides. "You don't understand," he said. "I've been to see half a dozen highly respected medical professionals in the last nine months. I even missed Christmas with my sister because one of those damn doctors suggested I spend a week in the desert learning meditation techniques."

The disgust in his voice made her grin. "That doesn't sound like you at all, no offense."

"None taken. The point is, no one thought my headaches were anything terribly serious until I went back for a second series of visits with my doctor here in Charleston. I wasn't getting any better. The senior radiologist read my MRI and CT scans. The report details were all there in black-and-white, Lisette. The doc told me flat out. I can't keep grasping for hope when there is none. I've decided to deal with this the best way I know how. If you can't live with that, then I'll simply hire a nurse when the time comes."

"And Tarleton Shipping?"

"Mazie will have to come up with a plan."

Lisette understood the futility of empty hope. She had certainly dealt with the phenomenon on multiple occasions during her mother's illness. But to imagine Jonathan dying was more than she could wrap her brain around.

"I'm sorry," she said quietly. "I won't mention it again."

"Thank you."

Once more she was struck by how alone he seemed. He did have family, but no one could walk this road with him. Her heart twisted. "I'll give you my answer Tuesday night, I swear."

Jonathan grimaced. "I shouldn't even be bringing you into this."

"I'm sort of the perfect choice," she said. "With my mother gone now, I have no demands on my time. We'll figure this out, Jonathan. We will."

His gaze seemed to settle on her lips. Or was it her breasts? "And you won't say anything to anyone?"

"No. It will be our secret, no matter what happens."

Five

Jonathan went home and hid himself away in his office, studying spreadsheets…making plans for a future he might not experience. More than anything, he wanted to talk to J.B. They had been best friends since grade school. J.B. wouldn't coddle him or shower him with false sympathy.

But once J.B. knew, there would be no keeping the secret from Mazie. Jonathan wasn't ready to break his sister's heart. The two of them had always been close, and they were even closer now that Hartley had abandoned the family.

Jonathan wrestled with unanswerable questions. How long did he have? Would he live to see Christmas? No matter how many novels he had read or movies he had seen, when the bitter news came to a man personally, it was a hell of a lot different from fiction.

He didn't want to die. He wanted to live.

Maybe the Tarletons had been cursed from the beginning. His mother's mental instability. His father's wavering health at a relatively early age. Hartley's betrayal. And now this.

Jonathan had read his share of pirate legends. Tales of buried treasures that were never found. The very spot of land on which the Tarleton home stood was reputed to have been the lair of the famous buccaneer Bloody Bart, an aristocratic Englishman who had been exiled to the New World after bringing shame to his family during a fatal duel.

Unlike the seventeenth-century pirate, Jonathan had nowhere to run. He would have to face his demons head-on.

After dinner with his father and a few games of chess, Jonathan escaped the house to walk the beach. The night was wild and windy, the tiny grains of sand scouring his exposed skin. The minor discomfort did not deter him.

Here in the privacy of his own company, he allowed himself to remember the afternoon with Lisette. Her home was warm and welcoming. Even walking through the front door had made him feel a sense of hope.

His reaction made no sense, not really. Hope was a commodity in short supply. He was a bastard for asking his executive assistant to give up months of her life to make *his* more palatable. She had been through so much.

But as guilty as he felt for involving her, he couldn't bring himself to rescind his request. He was bone-deep scared. He *needed* Lisette.

Her light and positivity and her ability to break monumental tasks into manageable pieces would keep him sane as uncertainty dogged his waking hours over the weeks and months to come. She would secure the Tarleton legacy, and thus give him peace.

The fact that Lisette had so matter-of-factly brought a potential physical relationship into the mix told him more than anything that he had been right in thinking she could handle what was to come.

Of *course*, sex would rear its head. A man and a woman. Legally wed. Friends who trusted each other and liked each other.

For his part, it was more than *like*. His body had responded urgently to her kiss. He didn't think he had ever before let on that he was attracted to her. At work, he had been scrupulously circumspect.

Yet when she bravely addressed the possible physical nature of their potential agreement, his libido had jumped in immediately. Reliving the moment when his lips claimed hers in a searing kiss made his breathing unsteady and his sex hard. If he had known what it would be like to hold her in his arms so intimately, he might never have been able to keep up the guise of boss and assistant as long as he had.

He craved Lisette.

Could he in good conscience allow their agreement to include physical intimacy? As much as he wanted to say, *Hell yes*, the more rational side of his brain urged caution.

If Lisette agreed to his unconventional proposal, both of their lives would change significantly. If they married, soon the world would look at both of them differently. Look and wonder...

Jonathan was hiding an enormous secret, and he had

demanded that Lisette keep his secret, too. He was expecting a lot from her. Some would say too much.

Still, when he imagined having her in his bed each night, the terrible weight that had rested on his shoulders when the doctor delivered the grim news seemed not quite so terrible. She would stand beside him when things got tough. She would have his back.

What did he have to offer her in return? She claimed not to care about his money, and from what he knew of her, that was certainly true. He'd tried to give her an unexplained bonus when her mother's medical bills mounted precipitously. Lisette had seen through his ruse and declined politely.

She was a proud woman. And self-sufficient. He had no idea what her financial circumstances were. Had her mother's extended illness been a monetary stress? And were there perhaps still bills outstanding?

Then and there, he decided on two of his nonnegotiable points for the prenup. First of all, he would pay off any of his new wife's debts, whether or not they stemmed from her mother's care. Secondly, he would buy Lisette a beach house…something relatively small and cozy and charming…with ample hurricane insurance to ensure that she would always be able to rebuild after any kind of natural disaster.

After those two decisions, his mental gyrations ground to a halt. What did he really know about his self-possessed assistant? Not much of a personal nature. Did she want to travel the world? Explore places off the beaten path? Take culinary lessons in France? Go back to school and get a doctorate in something?

He wanted to shower her with evidence of his gratitude, but he had no clue where to start. If he was successful in persuading her to marry him, perhaps his immediate goal should be to establish an emotional relationship with Lisette. Learn her likes and dislikes. Dig deep into the personality of a woman who was in many ways a mystery to him.

When his legs were aching, and his throat was dry with thirst, he finally turned around and made his way back home. Tuesday night. It seemed an eternity to wait.

Still, nothing good could come of this unless Lisette decided to help him of her own free will. No pressure from Jonathan. No emotional manipulation.

For a man accustomed to shaping the world and his destiny with bare hands and unflinching determination, this wait-and-see approach was sheer torment.

His customary store of patience had run out.

He wanted to call her right now. Show up on her doorstep again. Demand that she see things his way.

Instead, he let himself into the big, silent house, ate a cold roast beef sandwich and then climbed the stairs to his bedroom. He paused in the doorway, trying to view the masculine furnishings and dark colors from a female perspective. The first order of business would be to insist that Lisette redecorate. If she became his wife, this suite of room would be *theirs*, not his.

It was an important distinction.

The wind on his forehead during the beach walk had brought the headache back, but it was bearable. He showered and climbed beneath the covers.

Instead of contemplating his own demise, he closed his eyes and tried to recreate the memory of Lisette's lips beneath his. Her taste. The alluring shape of her body.

Physical arousal was almost a relief despite the lack

of a partner. How long would he feel like himself? He couldn't imagine a night where he slept beside his wife and didn't want to make love to her.

Groaning and cursing, he rolled to his stomach and buried his face in his arms. One slender woman held a great deal of his fate in her hands. She couldn't save him ultimately, but her answer would have a huge impact on how the next six months unfolded.

He knew what he wanted. Now he could only hope that she wanted it, too…

When Lisette arrived at work Monday morning, the boss was not in the building. No one seemed to know where he was, in fact.

She should have been relieved. Not having to face him meant she could get her work done. But her imagination ran amok. Had he suffered some kind of collapse? Was he regretting that he had shared his secret with her? Had his lawyer cautioned him about marriage under these circumstances?

Was Jonathan, even now, wondering how to tell her he had changed his mind?

By lunchtime he still had not made an appearance. No phone calls. No texts. No emails.

Only a visit from Rebekah managed to derail Lisette's escalating worry.

The other woman glanced at her watch. "You ready to eat? The cafeteria downstairs actually has a couple of good choices today."

Lisette shook her head. "I'd rather grab a yogurt and peanuts and take a walk, if you don't mind."

Rebekah was easygoing and cheerful. "Suits me,"

she said. "Let me get my sneakers out of my desk, and I'll meet you down front."

Thirty minutes later, warm and breathing hard, they found a shaded bench in the park and sat down to eat their brown bag lunches. Both of them had small fridges in their offices for just such an occasion.

Lisette's friend sighed, lifting her face to the leafy canopy overhead. "It's days like this I almost wish I were a carriage driver. I could spend the whole day outdoors."

"Sure you could. Educating grumpy tourists with history they don't care about. Wiping gum off the seats half a dozen times a day. Breathing horse sweat and car exhaust fumes."

Rebekah lifted both eyebrows. "Wow. What put you in such a prickly mood?"

"Sorry." Lisette grimaced. "I didn't sleep last night."

"You should try melatonin. I hear it works wonders."

Probably not under the current circumstances. "Maybe I will." Rebekah never had insomnia, to hear her tell it.

Her friend stood up and stretched. "I suppose we'd better be getting back. I hear the big boss frowns on slackers."

Her silly jest made Lisette squirm inwardly. "I wouldn't know. I've barely had time to breathe today. And that's with him MIA. It's worse when he's actually around. The man's brain never stops."

They took their time walking back. Rebekah tucked her sunglasses on top of her head when the sun went behind a cloud. She waved at a kid in a stroller and then glanced at Lisette. "Tamara and Nicole want us to get together soon and do some planning for the Alaska trip."

Lisette's heart dropped. How could she have forgotten? The four women had put down hefty deposits for a fabulous Inside Passage adventure in early September. "Um, I may have to bow out. Something has come up."

It was a clunky excuse at best. Rebekah stopped dead in the center of the sidewalk and gawked. "What are you talking about? This whole thing was your idea from the beginning."

It was true. Lisette had wanted to do something big and exciting to mark her new unencumbered lifestyle. She grieved her mother deeply, but for the first time in her adult life, she was now free to go and do and try things she had missed for so long. The Alaskan cruise had seemed like the perfect choice.

"It may seem crazy, and I don't know how to explain, but I can't be gone this fall."

"Why?" Rebekah's furrowed brow and perplexed expression were entirely justified.

"It's a secret," Lisette said weakly. "And it's not mine to tell."

Rebekah's face tightened with hurt. "I see."

"You don't," Lisette said urgently, taking her friend's arm. "I'd tell you if I could, but I swear it's important."

Rebekah pulled away. "You do realize that you sound ridiculous?" She shook her head in disgust and continued walking.

Lisette hurried to catch up. "I'll be able to tell you sometime, but not yet. Please don't be mad."

The Tarleton Shipping building loomed in front of them. Rebekah sailed through the front door without pause. They both boarded the elevator in silence. Unfortunately, three other employees stepped in as well. Purchasing was on the third floor. Lisette had to go all the way to the top.

When the quiet ding sounded and the doors slid open at three, Rebekah didn't say a word. Lisette's heart clenched. "I'll call you tonight," she said, trying not to sound desperate.

Rebekah's nod was curt. "Whatever."

And then the doors closed.

For the remainder of the afternoon, Lisette's stomach clenched in turmoil. This thing with Jonathan had blown up so quickly, she had not thought about the impact secrecy would have in her social circle. With no family to speak of except for a handful of distant cousins, her tight-knit group of friends in Charleston *was* her family. She couldn't afford to lose a single one of them over this charade, and certainly not Rebekah.

At four thirty, Jonathan still hadn't made an appearance.

Screw that. If the two of them were going to be partners in this terrible, sad experience, she wouldn't be pushed aside. Either she was central to Jonathan's life or she wasn't.

With her hands shaking, she pulled out her phone and sent a text to his private number. Where are you? I'm worried…

Ten minutes passed. Then twenty. She shut down her computer and tidied her desk. Anger and frustration began to edge out the worry. Jonathan couldn't expect her to be fully involved in his life and yet treat her like an afterthought. That wouldn't work. Period.

Just as she was about to head home, her phone finally dinged.

Sorry. I got a call before sunrise about a crisis at the New Orleans shipyard. They needed me on-site immediately. Everything has been resolved. I should be back in town before midnight.

Even as relief eased the knot in her chest, her misgivings grew. Was this the kind of thing Jonathan might expect her to handle in the upcoming weeks? She knew the workings of Tarleton Shipping inside and out, but that didn't mean she was adequately prepared to play his role. Her repeated assurances to him that she would be happy to help now made her feel trapped and anxious.

She wasn't the boss. Even if she married Jonathan, what did she know about imitating a man who was an alpha leader, a charismatic figure who could calm storms with his mere presence? Signing checks and directing meetings was one thing. But what about moments like today? Could she handle it?

All evening she brooded, wondering if it would be cowardly to back out. Jonathan was not alone. He had his sister and his father, and even his friend and brother-in-law, J.B.

Jonathan Tarleton wasn't without resources, emotional or otherwise.

Though it would seem cruel and unfeeling, she could still submit her letter of resignation. End the relationship. Walk away while she still had her pride and most of her heart.

Again she asked herself why Jonathan had suggested marriage. He claimed it was so that no one would question her legitimacy when she acted on his behalf. At some level, the explanation made sense. But what if he wanted marriage so he could manipulate her? Maybe he thought a legal union would give him more control.

In the privacy of her own home, her apprehension grew. After years of heavy responsibilities, she was now free to live her life on her own terms. Why would she give that up, knowing that to get entangled with Jonathan meant pain and heartache?

Deep in her heart, she knew why. She loved him desperately, and she wanted this time with him, however short it might be.

In the midst of her soul-searching, her cell phone rang. The number was all too familiar.

She hit the button. "Hello?"

Jonathan's voice rumbled in her ear. "It's me." He sounded tired.

"Are you home?"

"I am."

The stilted conversation was wince-worthy. He was her boss. She was his executive assistant. Despite their recent interactions, nothing had changed. Yet. She cleared her throat. "Did everything go well?"

"It did. Eventually. One of our foremen was accused of taking a bribe to use a Tarleton Shipping container for unlawful transport in exchange for drugs. The Feds were there. It was a huge mess. Fortunately, one of our solid guys reported what was about to happen. I've promoted him, by the way."

"Is he in danger now?"

"Thankfully, no. It wasn't some big international cartel. Just a local boy trying to make a buck."

"Ah. I'm glad it's over."

Silence fell.

Lisette jumped in before he could say anything else. "If you don't mind, Jonathan, I'd like to take the day off tomorrow. I have a lot to think about."

Six

Jonathan's gut clenched. He could hear it in her voice. She wasn't going to stick with him. Grinding his jaw, he tried to force normal, soothing words between clenched teeth. "Of course," he said. "Whatever you need."

"Thank you for being patient with me." Her tone was an attempt to placate him. The condescension only solidified the bleak disappointment that crushed his chest and made it hard to breathe.

"Why wouldn't I?" he said lightly. He wiped sweat from his brow and shrugged out of his jacket with his free hand. "I knew going into this that our potential agreement was a long shot. Your job isn't dependent on your answer. Surely you know that."

"I do," she said softly.

Damn, he hated telephone conversations. He wanted to see her face…read the expression in her eyes. Her irises were the light green of summer moss, but flecked with amber. Now that he thought about it, her eyes were definitely her best feature. A drowning man could find his way home in those eyes.

He glanced at the clock. "I should let you get to bed," he said gruffly. "It's late."

Lisette murmured her agreement and broke the tenuous connection.

The word *bed* hovered in Jonathan's brain like a symbol of all that was problematic with his marriage of convenience idea. Even given the definite spark between him and Lisette, she was not the kind of woman to enter into a casual relationship, marriage license or no marriage license.

He was momentarily taken aback to realize how very badly he wanted to see his ring on her finger. Were his feelings real, or was he creating an emotional connection in his brain to excuse the fact that he was trying to conscript her life to make his own easier?

It was too late to walk on the beach. Exhaustion rolled over him in a crushing wave. It was all he could do to shower and tumble into bed. Unfortunately, as soon as he turned out the lights, he began to see all the problems with his current situation.

Mazie and J.B. hadn't taken a real honeymoon back in January when they got married, because they were both tangled in business situations needing their attention. Now that things had settled down, his sister and his best friend had airline tickets and premium hotel reservations for a three-week getaway in Hawaii. They planned to leave Charleston the first of July. Mazie had talked about nothing else for days.

Originally, Jonathan had decided to tell them his

news when they got *home* from the islands. He didn't want to ruin their trip.

However, now, if there was any possibility Lisette was going to agree to marry him, he needed to talk to Mazie sooner than later. Jonathan sure as hell couldn't get married without telling his sister. She would be deeply hurt. Mazie would want to be there.

Could Jonathan do the wedding and save the bad news for later? Probably not. His sister would have too many questions about the speedy union.

His brain raced in circles. His head ached damnably despite the medication he had taken.

In an attempt to coax sleep, he shoved away all the questions about logistics and decisions and, instead, focused his thoughts on Lisette. A better man than he was would cut her loose. Absolve her of any responsibility for his future.

She deserved to be free. He had nothing to offer that would make up for the sacrifice she was considering. The fact that he was asking at all made him question his own honor.

Sleep came eventually. But it only visited in fits and starts, and was hardly restful. The following morning, he headed downtown an hour before his usual commute. Lisette wasn't going to be there. He needed to stay ahead of the curve today.

The hours dragged by.

He had a sandwich at his desk for lunch and continued working. Because he couldn't count on the future, he felt compelled to labor twice as hard as usual to make up for the uncertainty.

The only thing that sustained him throughout the afternoon when he wanted to sleep at his desk was the knowledge that Lisette would be with him tonight. She had promised.

At four there was a quiet knock on his office door. With no Lisette to stand guard, whoever it was had found him in his lair.

"Come in," he said.

The woman who entered was familiar... Lisette's friend. He gave her his best nonthreatening smile, because she seemed extremely nervous. "What can I do for you—Rebekah, isn't it?"

"Yes." She shifted from one foot to the other. "I'm sorry to intrude, Mr. Tarleton, but I'm worried about Lisette. She's been acting very odd lately, and she's not at her desk."

He winced inwardly, feeling more guilty than ever. His deceit was compounding expensive interest. "I'm sure she's fine," he said, perhaps a shade too heartily. "I would have heard if there were a problem."

"Oh." Rebekah hesitated. "Sorry I bothered you."

"No bother at all.

She smiled weakly and backed up. "Thank you."

Before he could say anything else, she was gone. Rebekah's visit was a stark reminder that Lisette had a life which didn't include Jonathan. He was asking a hell of a lot to drag his assistant into his personal crisis.

One glance at the clock told him he needed to leave. Earlier, he'd notified Lisette that he was sending a car service to pick her up at five thirty. Jonathan had exactly enough time to head home for a quick shower and change of clothes.

Oddly, now that the moment of decision was at hand, a feeling of peace wrapped him in calm. One way or another, tonight would give him the answers he needed.

By the end of the evening he would know if Lisette was prepared to help him.

If her answer was one he didn't want to hear, Jonathan would find his way alone.

Lisette decided, in retrospect, that taking the day off might not have been the answer to her problems. At least at work she would have been too busy to overthink the situation with Jonathan.

As it was, she ran five miles after breakfast, her apartment was now spotless and she had even baked a cake for the Tarleton Shipping receptionist whose birthday was tomorrow.

She had also spent far too much time wrangling with a decision that had no clear-cut answer.

The first hurdle in confronting the upcoming face-to-face with Jonathan was deciding what to wear. She had been to his beach house a hundred times. Tonight was different. Tonight was an occasion. Tonight she wanted to look her best.

Because there had been no let-up in the string of blistering, muggy days, she chose a pale green sundress splashed with poppies. It was new, and it was definitely not office attire. The fitted waist and flared above-the-knee skirt made her feel feminine and comfortable at the same time.

Cork-heeled taupe espadrilles with ribbons tied at the ankle completed her look. A bit of light makeup and she was done.

She hadn't argued when Jonathan offered to send a car to pick her up. Her nerves were shredded. Driving in this condition was not advisable.

At the Tarleton front gate, the driver lowered the

window so Lisette could punch in the code. Then he dropped her at the center of the driveway and departed the way he had come.

Lisette put a hand to her stomach, hoping she could even manage to *eat* dinner. She climbed the imposing curved staircase, pausing on the landing to admire the double mahogany doors inlaid with stained glass. Starfish and dolphins and sea turtles gamboled in bas-relief amid swirling hues of blue and green.

It occurred to her in an instant that if she married Jonathan, this would also be *her* house. The idea was bizarre…absurd. She was an ordinary person, the product of a single-parent home where money had always been tight, and an exciting evening out was popcorn and a movie.

This…this luxurious beachside mansion was the stuff of fantasy. Though she had worked here time and again when Gerald Tarleton or Jonathan needed her on-site, the prospect of being mistress of such a place was almost as daunting as that of being Jonathan's wife.

On an ordinary day, she would have used her key and let herself in. The senior Mr. Tarleton had mobility issues, and the chef and housekeeper were often too busy to play butler.

But tonight Lisette couldn't simply enter unannounced. This was Jonathan's home. The workday was over. He had invited her here for a special dinner to discuss his future…*their* future.

With her heart thumping like a wild bird in her chest and her hands damp, she rang the bell.

Moments later, Jonathan himself opened the door. His warm, intimate smile soothed some of her nerves. His gaze raked her from head to toe, missing nothing. "Lisette. Right on time. I hope you're hungry. Mrs. Rackham has outdone herself."

"The house smells amazing." As he stepped back to allow her to enter, she inhaled *his* familiar scent. Starched cotton. Warm male skin. A whiff of aftershave. The combination made her dizzy.

At the office, Jonathan invariably wore a suit. Despite Charleston's reputation for laid back hospitality, the head of Tarleton Shipping carried himself with formal reserve. Lisette often wondered if it was because he had inherited the helm of the business at a young age and needed to establish his dominance among employees who were often two decades his senior.

Tonight Jonathan was dressed more casually, though he still wore a navy sport coat over dark gray trousers and a crisp dress shirt. He'd done without a tie. Where the top buttons of his shirt were open, she glimpsed tanned skin and a hint of collarbone.

She had to remind herself to breathe.

"We'll go on into the dining room if that's okay with you," he said. "There's a cheese soufflé on the way, and I promised we wouldn't linger over drinks."

Lisette lowered her voice. "Well, since you *can't* drink and I'm not much of a wine connoisseur, I think we can live with that."

She caught her breath when she saw the table settings. Whatever instructions Jonathan had given the two ladies who ran his house so well had resulted in a spread worthy of the most elegant dinner party.

Fine, pale ivory china edged with silver. Heavy sterling flatware in an intricate pattern that looked as if it might have been antique. And a blush-pink linen tablecloth. In the center of all that magnificence sat a low crystal bowl overflowing with dahlias and white roses.

Jonathan held out her chair. "I hope you're hungry."

"I am now," she said, wondering if his fingers had brushed her bare shoulder by accident.

They were sitting at one corner of the table in a cozy arrangement that gave them both a spectacular view of the ocean. Jonathan lifted his crystal water glass. "To new beginnings."

She touched her goblet to his, meeting his bland gaze with suspicion. If this largesse was supposed to sway her decision, it was doing a great job. A woman could get used to this. "To the future," she said quietly. "May it be long and happy."

A shadow crossed his handsome face but was gone in an instant. He seemed determined to make the evening more social than serious. Lisette was okay with that. For the moment.

The meal was fabulous, as good or better than anything she had ever enjoyed at one of Charleston's many fine restaurants. Jonathan was a master at conversation. He'd learned at his father's knee perhaps. The fate of poor Mrs. Tarleton was somewhat of a mystery. She was still alive. That much Lisette knew. But rumor had it that she lived somewhere far away in a mental facility.

By the time dessert rolled around—coconut cream pie in a featherlight crust—Lisette had relaxed enough to actually enjoy herself. It was rare that she spent an evening like this with a man who was both intelligent and charming and far too sexy for his own good.

Her recent blind date couldn't compare.

As the housekeeper began to clear the table, they

stood. Jonathan took Lisette's elbow in a light touch and steered her toward the den.

Here, too, huge windows brought the outdoors inside. A fat, golden-red sun had begun its descent toward the horizon, though it was still several hours until dark.

"I've always loved this room," she said. "You're lucky to have grown up here."

"I probably take it for granted more than I should."

She couldn't read his expression. When she sat on the sofa, Jonathan remained standing, though not in one place. He paced restlessly, his body language jerky and uncoordinated, very different from his usual suave sophistication.

Her heart twisted. "If you've changed your mind, Jonathan, it's okay. Really. I won't be insulted."

He stopped and glared. "I haven't changed my mind, though I could give you the same speech."

Lisette shook her head slowly. "I've done little else but think about your situation from the moment you told me. I'm still not convinced that marriage is the answer, but you know your company better than I. If you believe you need a wife to conceal your condition in the short term, I'm willing to help you."

He exhaled deeply, as though he hadn't been at all sure she was going to cooperate. "That's good to hear."

"It might be easier, though, to simply *pretend* we got married. There wouldn't be as many layers of complication."

He stood at the window, his back to her. "The legalities are important." After a long moment of silence, he came and joined her, but on the opposite end of the couch. "If you're acting as my stand-in, the decisions you make will have to be binding."

"I hadn't considered that." After all, this was exactly why he needed her. To handle the reins of Tarleton Shipping when the CEO became too ill to function. The prospect speared her with regret and pain. "How long will you wait to tell your family?"

Jonathan grimaced. "I know it has to be soon. But I don't want to hurt them. I don't want to disrupt their lives."

She slipped off her shoes and propped her arm on the back of the sofa, head on her hand. "You're not God, Jonathan. You can't protect them from this. They're adults. Part of the way they'll cope is by being there for you when things get difficult. I understand it's hard. Being in control is who you are. You like taking charge. You're the boss."

"You say that like it's a bad thing." His joke fell flat.

"I *get* being a control freak. Honestly, I'm right there with you. During my mother's extended illness, I had to learn that setting impossibly high expectations for myself and life in general was a huge stress producer." She paused, uncertain how he would take her next words. "You're ill, Jonathan. You'll have to let down your guard, your reserve, for people to help you."

His dark frown told her he hadn't completely come to terms with what was ahead of him. "I hear what you're saying. I'll try. That's all I can promise."

"Fair enough."

His fingers tapped a restless rhythm on his thighs, drawing attention to the beauty of his fit body. The seemingly relaxed masculine sprawl made her want to scoot across the cushions that separated them and curl up in his lap.

She had to keep telling herself this was business. Or

at the very least, her good deed for the year. Her stupid crush would only complicate matters. She had to ignore the fact that she wanted Jonathan to fall in love with her.

The *loving* thing for her to do was keep her feelings in check and concentrate on him and what he needed. But what about her needs? Did she dare open up to him about what she really wanted? He was in a mood to offer her the moon. Maybe this was her chance to make part of her dreams come true.

Suddenly, he leaned forward and put his head in his hands. "I owe you an apology," he said, sighing.

"I don't understand."

"Your friend. Rebekah. She came looking for you and was pretty upset that you hadn't let her know you were going to be out of the office today. I didn't think about the ramifications of asking you to keep my secret."

"Oh." Lisette gnawed her lip. "She's bummed because I backed out of a trip we had planned for the fall. I couldn't explain. I suppose my not being at work today only compounded her confusion."

He sat up and frowned again. "Why would you cancel your vacation?"

Lisette stared at him. "For one, I can't take off on a girl trip if I just got married to you, and more importantly, September is three months from now. A lot of things could change."

She saw on his face the parade of emotions. First, the realization that she was right and, second, a grim distaste for having to plan an uncertain future. His jaw worked. "I want you to bring her in on the secret. You'll need someone, too, Lisette. For support. I'll ask her to sign a nondisclosure agreement."

"Thank you," she said quietly. "I wouldn't want to lose my best friend over this."

"I'm sorry I didn't look at your perspective sooner. I don't mean to be selfish. This entire situation has turned me into someone I barely know."

Lisette felt an urgency to reach out in this moment. She leaned toward him and touched his arm. "We're both finding our way, Jonathan. You're not a selfish person. Not at all. No matter how off kilter you may feel, you're the same man I've always admired and respected."

Seven

Jonathan jerked away, angry and embarrassed. It didn't help that Lisette looked as if she had stepped out of a spring garden. A man in his prime should be anticipating a night of pleasure with an appealing, sexy woman. Not preparing to go over dry legal documents.

But legal documents were the reason Lisette was here.

The concern in her eyes felt like acid on a raw wound. He didn't want her sympathy and her kindness.

He was a man, damn it. He wasn't weak, and he wasn't helpless.

"I'll get the paperwork," he said curtly, wishing he could put an end to this. He leaped to his feet and strode across the room to the armoire that discreetly disguised the television and other devices. Instead of keeping the documents in his home office where someone might have stumbled upon them today, he had stashed them in a shallow drawer that held batteries and extra cords.

The legal-size folder was cream colored with the name of his lawyer's firm embossed in gold. Even the weight of it in his hand felt momentous. He glanced over his shoulder at Lisette. "Shall we go to the office where you can spread out the papers and read them carefully?"

She shook her head, patting the seat beside her. "The coffee table will work. Why don't you come sit by me so you can explain stuff? Besides, I trust you. I don't have to read every word."

"Well, you should," he grumbled. "You're far too trusting."

Her gaze narrowed. "I told you I don't want your money. So there's nothing for me to worry about, now is there?"

Her snippiness restored his sense of humor. "Duly noted." He sat down beside her and was immediately assailed by an array of sensory delights. Her hair smelled like lemons. Her bare knees peeking out from beneath the hem of her sweet yet sexy dress struck him as unbearably erotic.

He cleared his throat and opened the folder, leaning forward slightly to place it in front of her on the polished wooden surface. "Take your time," he said. "There's lots of legal speak, but I think most of it is understandable in context. Let me know if you have questions."

Lisette leaned forward as well. They were sitting hip to hip. In better days, the two of them had gone over contracts together a hundred times. But never one like this.

Staring down at the sheaf of papers did little to distract his attention from how close she was…how good she smelled. Lisette was a *woman*. A woman he was hoping to marry.

For convenience, surely. And because she *could* and *would* keep his secret. But, try as he might, attempting to look at this situation as just another legal transaction didn't compute.

It was clear to him she was at least skimming the contents of the document and making note of the headings. He had included a generous posthumous settlement for his widow-to-be, as well as monthly payments to her personal account for the time that she would be his wife.

The lengthy silence on her part unsettled him. Perhaps the reality of seeing everything laid out in black-and-white was causing second thoughts.

At last she closed the folder, sat back and gave him a long, searching stare. "You can't give me five million dollars in exchange for six months of my life." The tone was flat.

"Of course I can. And we both know it might be longer than six."

Lisette's eyes flashed. "Six, twelve, eighteen…it doesn't matter. Your inheritance should go to your sister. Or your brother. Or both."

His fists clenched. "Hartley gets nothing from me. If you want to be noble and stupid, you can give your share to him. But not until I'm dead and gone."

"Do you know how irrational you sound when the subject of your brother comes up?"

Now his jaw was as tight as his fists. "Stay out of this, Lisette. I mean it. It has nothing to do with you."

"So I'll be your wife, but not really? You're the one who told me I would be family. Was that a lie?" Her dark gaze judged him and found him wanting.

"Quit twisting my words. You know what I mean."

"What happens if I don't sign your precious prenup?"

"Then no marriage."

Her jaw dropped the tiniest bit. Just enough to make him want to kiss those soft pink lips that had formed a tiny O of surprise. "But you need me."

He nodded. "I do. On my terms, though. My honor and my reputation are very important to me. In the end, that's all a man really leaves behind. If you choose to do this enormous, crazy thing for me, I'm determined to take care of you, Lizzy, even from the grave."

During his admittedly pompous speech, her eyes grew bigger and bigger. Moisture sheened that beautiful sea-glass green gaze. "I keep thinking this isn't real," she whispered.

His throat tightened, making it hard to speak. "So do I."

"Oh, Jonathan." She wrapped her arms around him, obviously seeking to offer comfort.

But he was far beyond being pacified by a simple hug. He craved the oblivion of physical passion. With his heart slamming in his chest, he rested his chin on top of her head.

Then, because his self-control was tenuous at best under the circumstances, he eluded her embrace and stood. His forehead was damp with sweat. His mouth was dry. "There's nothing in the contract about physical intimacy. I want you to have time to get to know me. To decide if a *marriage* in every sense of the word is something you want. But those considerations are strictly between you and me. Whether or not we decide to live together as man and wife in the same bed, the terms of the contract are binding."

Lisette stood as well. In her bare feet, she seemed small and vulnerable. Yet the woman he knew so well was resilient and resourceful.

He followed her when she went to the window, though he kept a safe distance between them. The ocean was gray and dark now, painted with a vivid stripe of gold and red cast by the sun trying valiantly to stay above the horizon. The room was becoming dim. No one had turned on a light.

Lisette shrugged. "In other circumstances, I might have enjoyed becoming your lover."

With her back to him, she couldn't see his shock. "And now?" he asked, the words strained.

She whirled and leaned against the glass, her arms crossed below her breasts. "I don't want to fall in love with you and have my heart broken."

Disappointment flooded his chest. "I see."

"I doubt you do. You're an extremely handsome man. I'm sure that any number of women have wanted to seduce you. And yet I don't even know if you've been in a serious relationship recently."

"I haven't," he said brusquely. "Nothing but work and family. I'm a very dull boy."

She rolled her eyes. "Nice try." After a hushed breath, she let her gaze slide over him from head to toe. As if she were sizing up an item she meant to purchase. It was not the look of an innocent who was curious. Nor was it particularly flirtatious. Instead, her frank assessment was intense. Personal.

Her shoulders lifted and fell, drawing attention to creamy skin and a delicate collarbone. "I think you forgot something."

He lifted an eyebrow. "Surely not. My lawyer is very thorough."

Lisette actually chuckled. The feminine sound made the back of his neck tingle. "You told me I could ask for anything I wanted," she said. "Don't you remember?"

"Ah, yes. The orange M&M's. Is that it?"

She shook her head slowly, pale green eyes filled with a million secrets he couldn't decipher. "Of course not."

"Then what?"

As he stared at her, half aroused, half alarmed, her tongue came out and wet her lips. In that moment, he realized she wasn't calm at all.

"Lisette?" He prompted her, trying to break the long gap in the conversation.

She shrugged, her expression both wary and intent. "I want you to give me a baby."

Lisette winced when Jonathan actually stumbled backward a step, his shock almost palpable. When he didn't respond, her stomach clenched, and her face and throat burned. "Say something," she muttered, mortified that she had actually gone through with her proposition. The idea had come to her in the middle of the night. At 3:00 a.m., it had even made perfect sense.

"Umm…" Jonathan rubbed his chin where the faint shadow of dark beard said he might not have shaved since early morning. She liked the way he looked. A lot.

"That's not an answer."

He cursed beneath his breath. "Good Lord, Lisette. You can't drop a bomb like that and expect an immediate response. Is this for real?"

"Of course it's for real," she snapped. "I don't go around asking men to get me pregnant for the heck of it."

"But why?"

His befuddlement made her angry. "You have no clue, do you? I'm thirty-seven, Jonathan. Five years older than you, almost five and a half."

"Five years is nothing."

"Says the man who's not even thirty-two. I've spent all of my adult life caring for my mother. Thankfully, she's at peace and no longer in pain. I'm free to make a life for myself. But there's no significant other on the horizon, and now I'm contemplating being with you for a year, give or take. My stupid biological clock is ticking. I don't think I should wait any longer."

"A baby..." He said it with wonderment and concern as if he actually had no idea at all how the process started.

"It's not so farfetched," she said quietly. "You're a decent man, and if I did get pregnant, you could look at it as leaving a piece of yourself behind."

His face darkened. "It? The baby? It wouldn't be an *it* though, would it? Your baby would be mine, too. A precious little one I'd love. And grieve all the more to have to say goodbye. What you're asking isn't fair, Lizzy."

She hadn't thought of it in those terms. Of course he would love a baby. And not living to see his own child grow up would be a terrible burden to bear.

Still, something inside her said this was the perfect time, the perfect man, her last chance.

Was she fooling herself to think she wouldn't come to love Jonathan exponentially more as his wife, as the mother of his child? How could she bear it? Unless, when her heart was broken and aching at losing Jonathan, she could find comfort in a baby... a tiny version of him to love.

"I suppose not," she said, trying to put herself in his shoes. "But promise me you'll think about it. I wouldn't ask if it wasn't important to me. Very important, Jonathan."

He nodded slowly, his expression grim. "I promise. Though I have to be honest with you… I can't imagine changing my mind. My sister and brother-in-law are struggling to get pregnant. What would they think if I deliberately tried to get *you* pregnant knowing I won't live to raise my own child?"

"If they eventually conceive, this baby…*our* baby… would be a cousin. That's special and sweet."

He shook his head slowly. "You make a persuasive argument. I'll think about it. I can't give you more than that."

She nodded, though something told her he wouldn't be easy to convince. "Hand me something to write with. Let's do this, and then I don't want to see these papers ever again."

Jonathan's expensive fountain pen was weighty in her hand. She signed her name again and again…everywhere a small yellow flag denoted her input. Finally, she capped the pen, straightened the papers and closed the folder.

Her husband-to-be had stared at her the entire time as if afraid she might bolt. Now he smiled. "You're doing a good thing, Lisette. I'm grateful. I swear you won't regret it."

That was a vow he likely couldn't keep. She felt sick with nerves. She was signing her life away in order to watch the man she cared for deeply abandon her in death. She was in love with him, planning to build a life—albeit temporary—with him, and then would ultimately watch it disappear. Was she crazy to go through with the marriage?

But then again, life in general was nebulous and uncertain. She had to take this chance. "What next?" she asked quietly.

"I've spoken to the judge. He's a family friend. We can get married in his chambers Saturday morning."

She sucked in a breath. "So soon?"

"No reason to wait."

"Will it be just you and me?"

"We'll need witnesses. You'll bring Rebekah. I'll have Mazie and J.B."

"Which means we have to tell them tomorrow."

"Yes."

"And what about your father?"

For once, the decisive head of Tarleton Shipping appeared unsure. "I'm still wrestling with that one. Most days he's fine, but his mental faculties slip in and out. I'm not sure he'd be capable of keeping either secret— my health *or* the real reason for the marriage. I think it may be best not to say anything at all to him for the time being."

"Don't you think he'll notice someone new is living in his house?"

Her sarcasm rolled off Jonathan without hitting its mark. "Dad's quarters are on the main floor. He won't have a clue what you and I are doing upstairs."

Suddenly, a startling vision flashed in her brain. Jonathan's bed. The two of them naked between the sheets. Her breathing quickened. "People will expect us to take a honeymoon," she said, trying not to think about what traditionally happened on post-wedding trips.

"True." He frowned. "I suppose we could go somewhere for a few days."

"Or simply say that things at work are too busy for you to be gone right now…that we're planning a big romantic getaway for later in the year."

"Unfortunately, we just finished a series of seminars on work/life balance. Remember?"

"Ah…" He was right. Jonathan was a great employer. The benefits package at Tarleton Shipping was second to none. He encouraged his staff to take their vacation days…all of them. Research underscored that a happy, well-rested work force was more productive.

How would it look if the boss himself didn't even take time off to get married?

Jonathan punched something into his phone. "A week in the Caribbean should do it, don't you think?"

She blinked. "The Caribbean?"

"One of my buddies owns a villa in Antigua. He's offered it to me half a dozen times. Comes complete with a household staff. Nothing to do but relax in the sun. I just sent him a text."

"Wouldn't it be booked by now?"

"Maybe not this time of year. Winter is high season."

Seven days and nights in a tropical paradise with a fake husband who just happened to be her boss. What could possibly go wrong?

Before she could come up with a believable objection, Jonathan's phone dinged. He held it up triumphantly. "We're in for the entire week. He says the days are available."

"Do you really want to be gone that long?" Jonathan rarely took any time for himself.

He dropped his phone on the desk. "We need this,

Lizzy. A chance to get used to each other away from prying eyes. The fiction of a honeymoon will make things that much easier when we go back to work."

Now he crossed the room and took her shoulders in his hands. His thumbs caressed her collarbone. He was so close she couldn't breathe.

"That makes sense, I suppose," she said.

"Look at me, Lisette."

Reluctantly she tipped back her head and met his brown-eyed gaze straight on. "What now?"

"You don't seem like a woman who's excited about taking a break from work."

"I haven't taken a real vacation in a very long time. I'm not good at relaxing. A definite character flaw."

"Are you worried because I'll be with you?"

She felt naked beneath his intent stare. "I'm sure we can do our own thing and not get in each other's way."

His chest rose and fell in a mighty sigh. He tucked her hair carefully behind her ears. Then he pressed a gentle kiss to her lips. "Thank you, Lisette. For everything."

Her immediate instinct was to pull back. Not because she didn't want the kiss, but because she wanted it far too much.

But she didn't jerk away, and she didn't refuse his overture. This was the man she was going to marry on Saturday.

When she kissed him back, he was the one who seemed startled.

He made a noise low in his chest. A groan. Then two big hands came up and cupped her cheeks. "God, you're sweet," he muttered.

The kiss deepened. Lisette allowed herself to relax in his embrace, to enjoy the novelty of having a man—

this man in particular—hold her and let her know without words that he wanted her. She felt the urgency of his arousal.

Men could enjoy sex without involving their emotions. She knew that. Even so, Jonathan's desperation slid beneath her defenses and made her believe this marriage might have a chance of becoming real.

His tongue moved between her lips and stroked hers, taking the starch out of her knees and stealing her breath. Her arms encircled his neck. Her fingertips found the silky hair at his nape and played with the baby-fine strands.

Jonathan took the kiss deeper, more dominant now, less afraid perhaps that she might not want what he had to offer...that she might not want him.

She moaned, pressing ever closer. She wanted this and so much more. But how could she protect herself?

Suddenly, she saw the clock on the wall behind his shoulder. Like Cinderella, her time was up. She pulled away, smoothing her hair awkwardly. "I have to go," she said. "The driver will be waiting at the gate."

"You asked him to come back? Why? You knew I would take you home." His frown was black.

"I wasn't entirely sure how the evening would go," she confessed. "It seemed better this way."

"You're afraid of me?" He was visibly insulted.

She touched two fingers to his lips, lingering there for a moment before stepping back from temptation. "I was afraid of us," she said.

Eight

The next day, Jonathan sat opposite his sister and his best friend and watched them process the news. He'd tried to phrase things diplomatically. He'd wanted to spare them the worst of what he knew. But despite his best efforts, it was what it was. The end.

Mazie wept openly. J.B.—his arm around his wife—looked as if he'd been kicked in the chest by a horse.

The three of them had just finished dinner. When Jonathan had phoned his sister and told her he wanted to come over, she had insisted on cooking…claimed she rarely had the chance anymore.

Her business kept her tied up most days.

Now they all sat in the beautifully appointed living room with the veranda that overlooked Meeting Street, and Mazie cried.

J.B. cleared his throat. "Are you sure?"

It was the same question Lisette had asked in the beginning. Maybe it was the question all families asked when faced with a difficult diagnosis. A plea for a help and a way out.

Jonathan nodded. "I'm sure. Multiple doctors. Multiple tests. I didn't want to tell you both yet. I didn't want to ruin your trip. But Lisette insisted."

J.B. narrowed his eyebrows. "Lisette?"

"His executive assistant," Mazie croaked, wiping her eyes.

"I know who she is. Nice lady. Smart enough to keep *Jonathan* in line."

"I hope so," Jonathan said. "Because I'm marrying her on Saturday. And I need you both to be there."

J.B. snorted. "Has your brain started shutting down? You can't get married Saturday. That's ridiculous."

Mazie slugged her husband's arm. "Not funny." Then her expression faltered. "But I don't understand, Jonathan. You've never given me any hint that you thought of Lisette romantically. Besides, isn't she quite a bit older than you?"

He shrugged, irritated by that same stupid argument. "Five years. It's not a big deal. But no. We're not in love. I asked her to marry me so I could appoint her as a partner in the company. As my health fails, Lisette will be deputized to make decisions. And in the short term, she can cover for me if I have bad days. It's imperative that we stave off news of my illness as long as possible so our stock prices aren't affected."

J.B. folded his arms across his chest, for once his expression deadly serious. "What's to keep her from ruining you financially? I have some experience in this arena. How well do you know her? Can she be trusted?"

Jonathan reached for patience. J.B.'s first wife had been in it for the money and had made his life a misery. It was understandable that J.B. had issues when it came to women and marriage.

"I'd trust her with my life," Jonathan said. "I suppose I literally am. But there's a prenup, so you can stand down. I love you both, and I want you to be with me Saturday when I tie the knot. The only other person who's going to know the whole truth is Lisette's best friend. Rebekah will there, too."

Mazie stood and wrapped her arms around him. His baby sister's tight hug threatened to shake Jonathan's hard-won composure.

"So do I throw you a big reception?" she asked, the words muffled against his shirt. Her wet face had dampened the fabric.

He leaned his cheek on the top of her head. "Thanks, sis, but no. We're heading off immediately for a honeymoon in Antigua. I want the whole newlywed thing to look as real as possible."

J.B. stood as well, grim faced. "What if your health takes a bad turn when you're out of the country?"

Jonathan straightened and patted Mazie on the back. He didn't need sympathy right now. He needed everyone to treat him like normal; otherwise, he'd never make it through these next few months.

"It won't be that fast, according to the doc. Even the headaches have been irregular. Some days I feel fine."

"But you're definitely *not* fine." His sister pulled herself together visibly. "We should contact Hartley."

"No." Jonathan shouted the word, his neck tight with rage and the deep hurt he had felt ever since his brother's betrayal. At Mazie's stricken expression, he tempered his tone. "I can't deal with him right now. I'll need all my energy to keep the company afloat and to deal with whatever physical symptoms come my way. My brother is not part of the equation. Promise me you won't try to contact him, Mazie."

He could see the struggle on her face. At last she nodded. "If that's what you want. And Daddy?"

Jonathan shook his head. "I have no idea. He'll have to be told…eventually. But I think in these early days it's best to pretend everything is normal."

"You're probably right."

The three of them stood there in a small circle. For a moment, Jonathan could almost glimpse the children they had been so long ago. These were two of the most important people in his life.

He sighed. "I want you to be kind to Lisette. This will be extremely difficult for her. She'll need your support and friendship."

"I wasn't going to run her out of town," J.B. groused. "But I'm still not comfortable with you giving her so much power."

Mazie patted her husband's hand. "We'll have dinner together. You'll see how great she is." She glanced at her brother. "As soon as you get back? We won't go to a restaurant, though. It needs to be here. So we can talk freely."

"I'd like that, Maze," Jonathan said. "Honestly, right now I'm taking things one day at a time. It's not a great feeling."

The conversation gradually moved to other topics, but Jonathan wasn't fooled. His illness was the enormous elephant in the room.

The news had changed both his sister and his best

friend. Mazie was shocked and subdued and very upset, but trying not to show it. J.B.—who was the life of any party—had morphed into an unusually serious man, one with pain in his eyes.

Jonathan struggled with inexplicable guilt. He was strong. He would handle whatever was coming. But hurting the people he loved was a consequence no number of pep talks could soothe.

As the evening wore on, he realized he needed to leave them alone to process the difficult news he had shared. Besides, it was late, and he was exhausted. Not from any physical exertion today. But from the effort to carry on as normal when his emotions were all over the map.

He didn't want emotions. He didn't trust them. From the time his father had tucked his so-very-ill mother away in an institution, Jonathan had learned that life was easier when he bottled up all his pain and refused to acknowledge its existence.

J.B. walked him down to the car. The two men stood in silence beneath the neon glow of a security light.

J.B.'s expression was equal parts angry and determined. "Are you holding anything back? You can protect Mazie, but I won't have you lying to me, even if you think you have a damned good reason."

Jonathan leaned against the car, jingling keys in his hand. "Swear to God, that's it. No cure. No hope. And worst of all, no timetable. They'll repeat my scans every two months. So we'll know where things are."

"Son of a bitch." J.B.'s vehement curse was weirdly helpful. It expressed the utter outrage and incredulity Jonathan felt, the gut-level response he hadn't allowed himself.

"I'm heading home," he said. "Dad will wonder why I'm so late."

"And your bride-to-be? What about her?"

"We'll see each other at work in the morning. Back off, J.B. She's doing a wonderful thing for me."

"And she'll be a wealthy widow in the end."

The sarcasm wasn't veiled. Jonathan's temper boiled. "Of course she will. Because that's the way I want it. I have no idea how this is all going to go down. I asked a woman who's been through hell with her own mother to do it all over again. That makes me the villain in this scenario, not Lizzy."

"Lizzy? You're cozy enough for nicknames?"

"We've worked together a long time. We're friends."

"Just friends?" J.B. didn't bother to hide his skepticism. "Or is there more to this than you wanted Mazie to know? Have you and your executive assistant hooked up now and again?"

"Not that it's any of your damned business, but no. It's not like that."

"Sorry, bud. You don't sound convincing at all. I'm guessing you have a *thing* for her, and when your world got caught up in this wicked undertow, your subconscious grabbed onto the nearest lifeline."

Jonathan sucked in a sharp breath. J.B. had known him since they were both five years old. J.B. was smart and extremely perceptive, despite his genial, good-ole'-boy demeanor. There might be a kernel of truth in his summation of the current situation.

"Well, hell."

J.B. chuckled, this time with no sympathy at all. "You want her, don't you?"

Jonathan rubbed the back of his neck. "I'd be lying if

I said I hadn't fantasized about her now and again. But I swear I never stepped over any line at work. Never. Not once."

"Settle down. I believe you. But the bigger question is, what does Lisette think about you?"

"Hell if I know. She has a big heart. And she feels sorry for me."

"It wouldn't be entirely surprising if she had a thing for you. Some women go for the buttoned-up, way-too-serious type."

Jonathan choked out a rusty laugh. Trust J.B. to make him see the humor in a dire situation. "Thanks for the ringing endorsement."

"When you remember to smile and you tear yourself away from spreadsheets and budgets, you're not half-bad."

"I'll put that on my tombstone."

"Shit, Jonathan. This can't be happening." In a completely atypical move, J.B. grabbed him close and gave him a crushing bear hug. "I'm here for you, man, day or night. You know that, right?"

Jonathan pulled away, both deeply touched and deeply despairing. "I do."

They stood there in silence, forever it seemed, neither of them willing to walk away. J.B. finally cursed beneath his breath. "If I fly in another specialist, will you see him or her? I've got the money. You know I do."

"And so do I. Your generosity is duly noted. But I swear I've seen the best. No one thought the headaches were anything serious, because they come and go. I'm healthy as a horse by any other metric. It took this last round of tests to get at the truth. My doctor is a professional. It's hard to miss a giant fucking tumor…" His voice cracked embarrassingly.

J.B. stared at the ground, and then his jaw thrust out the same way it had every time he'd been thwarted as a kid. "You're the best damn man I've ever known, hands down. If there's even a shred of a chance, you'll find it. I'd lay money on it."

Jonathan's eyes burned. "Oh, crud, J.B. If this is some kind of wind-beneath-my-wings speech, quit embarrassing yourself. Besides, I'm not riding off into the sunset yet."

"We're a team, bro. Wherever it takes us."

The team had once included Hartley. Jonathan shoved the random, painful thought aside. "I'll see you Saturday," he said gruffly.

"We'll be there."

"I'll text Mazie the details."

"You know she's going to smother you, don't you? The woman is a born nurturer."

"She definitely is. No news on the fertility front?"

"Not yet. But it's early. We're supposed to relax. The doctor says that's important."

"It will happen."

"I think so, too."

"I wish I could have kept this from her. The worry can't be good when she's trying to get pregnant."

"Mazie would have killed you herself if you'd kept her in the dark and she found out. We'll be fine."

Jonathan climbed into his car, started the engine and lowered the windows. Immediately, the scent of roses seeped into the hot interior. "Take care of my sister, J.B."

His friend's nod was curt. "Always."

* * *

Thursday morning at ten, Lisette brought Rebekah downstairs in front of the Tarleton Shipping building to meet Jonathan. After a brief, awkward round of greetings the three adults piled into Jonathan's car. Lisette sat in the back with Rebekah.

When Lisette's eyes met Jonathan's in the rearview mirror, his intense gaze made her stomach flip. Yesterday had seemed a million years long. Though Jonathan had been in and out of the office, they barely spoke to each other. She knew he had met with his sister and brother-in-law last night, but she hadn't found the opportunity to quiz him about how things had gone.

And as for Rebekah… Lisette's poor friend was confused and apprehensive and trying not to show it. All Lisette had been able to tell her was that she was going to be brought in on some company secrets and that it would require her to sign a nondisclosure agreement.

The trip to the lawyer's office was little more than ten minutes, even in traffic. Jonathan's lawyer was an extremely attractive blonde who might have been Lisette's age. Maybe even a bit older. After she greeted Jonathan, he volunteered to step into an outer office while the three women met.

Lisette appreciated his courtesy. Rebekah's eyes had grown wider and rounder with every step of the process. She would be more comfortable without the head of Tarleton Shipping in the room.

When the three women were alone, the lawyer jumped right in. "Thank you for coming today, Rebekah. Jonathan and Lisette want to share some information with you, but the subject matter is sensitive. If you choose not to be brought in at a higher level, you may say so, and we won't go any further."

Rebekah looked at Lisette. "Do you need me to do this?"

For a moment, Lisette felt the weight of guilt. Keeping secrets was not easy. She desperately wanted to be able to talk to her friend about all that was going on. "I do," she said. "We've always shared everything. This is important, or I wouldn't ask."

Rebekah turned back to the lawyer. "Give me the papers. I'll sign whatever Lisette wants me to."

The document was at least a dozen pages long... legal-size pages. The lawyer flipped; Rebekah signed again and again.

When it was done, the lawyer gathered the document into a folder. "I'll have my staff make copies. Each of you will receive one, as will Jonathan." Her businesslike demeanor softened. "I'll leave you two to talk for a few minutes. With the door closed, no one will disturb you."

The room was silent. Rebekah put her hands to her flushed cheeks. "Say something, please. I'm freaking out over here. I feel like I'm in a spy movie. What the heck is going on?"

Lisette started talking and couldn't stop. She hadn't realized what an enormous relief it was going to be to finally share the details of the past few days with someone who really cared and could actually help her work through the morass of personal and ethical dilemmas she faced.

When she explained Jonathan's illness, Rebekah looked stricken. "Oh, God. I'm so sorry."

"There's more," Lisette said. "He wants to keep the

news under wraps as long as possible so the company stock won't be affected."

Rebekah nodded. "That makes sense. And you're his assistant, so you'll have to be in the know." She paused, frowning. "But why me? What do I have to do with anything?"

Lisette chewed the inside of her lip until she tasted the tang of blood. "You thought I was acting weird and selfish, and rightly so. You're my best friend. I *needed* you to know so that our relationship wouldn't be in danger."

"But there's more, surely. I signed my life away a moment ago. What's it all about?"

Lisette couldn't sit still any longer. The lawyer's personal office was spacious and beautifully decorated, but there wasn't much room to pace. Lisette was shaky and tense. Saying these things out loud made her decision seem more real, more radically dangerous.

"Jonathan has asked me to marry him," she said slowly. "So that when his condition begins to deteriorate, I can make decisions and step in as his proxy."

Rebekah's expression intensified every one of Lisette's doubts. Her friend looked either incredibly shocked or horrified, or maybe a mixture of both. "That's insane," she said. "He can't ask that of you. It's too much."

"Well, he did," Lisette muttered. She had never breathed a word about her crush on her boss. As far as Rebekah knew, Jonathan was nothing more than an employer. "He'll be going through hell, Rebekah. I can't stand by and watch him suffer if I can help."

"What about his family?"

"They'll be supportive, of course. But because of my position, I'm uniquely suited to help him run Tarleton

Shipping. The fiction of our wedding will deflect any grumblings about why I'm being given so much latitude in decision-making."

"I still don't like it," Rebekah said, her gaze troubled. "It sounds like he's taking advantage of you. It's not fair."

If there was ever a time for truth, it was now. "I care about him, Rebekah."

"As a human being, you mean?"

"As a man. I love him. No matter how hard this is, I want to be with him for however long he has left."

Nine

Lisette's life became both easier and harder in the hours that followed. Easier, in that Rebekah was now her confidante, her sounding board. Harder, because the plan that had been set into motion accelerated rapidly.

Rebekah was tucked into a cab to return to the office without them. Lisette and Jonathan went to the courthouse for the marriage license.

Producing a photo ID and watching Jonathan hand over cash for the fee was certainly not romantic under the circumstances. Lisette felt the noose of inevitability tighten around her neck.

Any woman would want to marry a man like Jonathan. But the speed and the matter-of-fact way he was ticking off items on his list was a little too clinical for Lisette's taste. She wanted to be more to him than a convenience.

As she penned her name alongside his, her hand shook. The wet ink smudged, making her handwriting almost illegible. "Do we need to start over?" she asked the clerk.

The young woman shook her head. "Nope. It's still legal. That's all that matters."

Outside on the courthouse steps, Lisette paused to pull her sunglasses from her purse. The day was bright and sunny, but mostly she wanted to be able to hide behind them. With each moment that passed, she was becoming more and more aware of her handsome fiancé.

"Are we going to grab lunch?" she asked. "I'm starving. I was too nervous about Rebekah and the lawyer to eat breakfast."

Jonathan grimaced. "I'd love to, but I have a meeting. I can drop you at the office, though."

His gaze was trained on the throngs of tourists passing by on the street. Charleston was a popular vacation spot.

Once again his habitually aloof mask was firmly in place.

Lisette's heart sank. Was this how it was going to be between them? Cold and distant whenever he couldn't handle the emotional aspects of the situation? Suddenly, she couldn't bear to be near him. "I'll walk," she said curtly.

She took off down the steps at a breakneck pace, considering the fact that she was wearing heels. Tears stung her eyes. She blinked them away angrily. How could he treat her like nothing more than a coworker when he had begged her to marry him?

"Wait. Stop."

She ignored him, walking faster. Her throat and her

chest were tight. Forty-eight hours. She had forty-eight hours to decide if she could go through with this charade.

A large, masculine hand grabbed her shoulder, spinning her around. Jonathan tugged her into a patch of shade at the entrance to an alley. "I'm sorry," he said, his gaze contrite. "I've never been in this situation before. I'm making a mess of it. I don't know how I'm supposed to act." Without asking permission, he removed her sunglasses and wiped tears from beneath her eyes.

The stupid, dense man was so close they were breathing the same air. She felt naked without her polarized protection. "Give me those." She snatched for the sunglasses, but he held them away, out of reach. She glared at him. "Just pretend you're getting married for the *normal* reasons," she said, infusing the words with all the sarcasm she could muster. "Pretend some poor deluded woman actually cares about you." Her voice escalated to an embarrassing octave.

His gaze settled on her lips, the hot stare almost tangible. "And do you, Lisette? Do you care about me?"

"That's not a fair question," she mumbled, finally retrieving her sunglasses from his grasp. She settled them on her nose. "I need food. Go away."

Those gorgeous masculine lips quirked upward in a smile that stole her breath. "I care about you, Lizzy Stanhope. I have for a long time. In fact, I almost asked you out on half a dozen different occasions. But in the age of #MeToo, I decided it wasn't the thing to do. Because I had no clue if you were even interested."

"*Why* do you care about me? Or how?"

He shrugged. "You're cute and funny and smart. I enjoy your company."

His calm pronouncement destroyed her composure. The aloof Jonathan might be better for her in the long run. "I'm sorry I yelled at you," she said meekly. "You should go. You'll be late for your meeting."

He said a rude word, a word she'd never heard him use. Then he slid his hands beneath her hair and cupped her head. When he lowered his mouth to hers, his lips firm and warm and demanding, everything spun in a dizzying arc behind her eyes. Maybe she had heat stroke.

Was it possible for a really good kiss to short-circuit a woman's brain? When she finally regained her senses, Jonathan was breathing hard. His face was flushed. Her sunglasses were tucked in the breast pocket of his jacket. When had that happened?

She swallowed. "Was that supposed to be an apology?"

He grinned. "I don't know. Did it succeed?"

"Yes, damn you. But don't expect to bamboozle me so easily every time we get in an argument."

"*Bamboozle?* Maybe you *are* too old for me."

That he could tease her so easily moments after they had kissed each other senseless told her he felt comfortable with her. Or something. *Comfortable* was definitely a misnomer.

This crackling awareness between them was not exactly relaxing.

She waved a hand. "Go take care of business. I'm not mad at you. I know it's hard for a high-powered businessman to be gone for a week."

He glanced at his watch and muttered an imprecation beneath his breath. "I'll see you in the morning."

"Probably not. You're not the only one with plans to make."

"I stand corrected. At the courthouse then? Saturday? Two o'clock?"

"Yes. I'll be there."

He kissed her again, long and slow and sweet as honey. "Thank you, Lisette. I swear you won't regret it."

She already did, but that was grief for another day. In the here and now, she would pretend nothing was wrong. Putting her palms against his hard, warm chest, she shoved. "Go. We're good. I won't be a no-show. You don't have to worry about me, Jonathan."

Backing away slowly, he lifted a hand. "Saturday. Don't be late." Then he shifted into a loping run and disappeared around the corner.

Though Lisette and Rebekah were in the office for the remainder of Thursday, they each decided to burn a vacation day on Friday so Lisette could find a dress to wear for the wedding.

It was a tall order on short notice. Fortunately, Rebekah was a hard-core reader of glossy bridal magazines and a devotee of every wedding-themed show on TV. She picked up Lisette at nine the next morning and was prepared with a list of Charleston's boutiques and bridal salons to hit up.

Lisette couldn't help wishing her wedding was going to be different. She had always assumed that one day she would walk down the center aisle in a big church with violins playing "Pachelbel's Canon."

Grow up, kid, she lectured herself sternly. During the years of her mother's lengthy illness, she'd had to learn time and again that special occasions couldn't be planned too carefully. Circumstances dictated change. Life was unpredictable.

She thrust her girlish daydreams into a mental lockbox and reminded herself why she was really going through with this wedding.

Jonathan Tarleton needed her.

Forty-eight hours after the meeting in the lawyer's office, Jonathan stood in the judge's chambers and felt his pulse rate increase. Lisette was late. Not terribly so, but enough to tighten his stomach.

Mazie fiddled with the silk pocket square in his charcoal suit. "You look so handsome," she whispered. Tears filled her eyes and spilled over. "I know why you're taking this honeymoon, but I don't want you to go. I'll worry about you every minute of the day. Promise you'll call and text."

He kissed her forehead. "Of course I will. Besides, I'm feeling fine right now. Haven't had a headache in three days."

"You don't have to be brave for me." She put her arms around him. "Hartley should be here. It's not right."

"Don't start with me, Maze. Today is hard enough without you heaping sentimental guilt on my head."

She pulled back, looking hurt. "You're my brother and I love you, but sometimes you are so damn stubborn I could smack you."

He pinched her chin, a maneuver she had hated since childhood. "That goes both ways, little chick."

J.B. waved an arm between them. "Hey. Break it up, you two. I think the bride has arrived."

Jonathan spun and watched the door swing open wide. Rebekah entered first, wearing a flattering summer dress that was the green of Lisette's eyes. Behind her stood the woman who made his heart race. A wide-eyed, pink-cheeked bride-to-be. His feet carried him across the room, though he didn't remember telling them to move.

"Lizzy," he muttered, stunned and moved. "You look amazing."

Her wedding gown was exactly right. Not too casual and not too traditional. It was perfect for a marriage of expedience in a judge's office. The ivory lace made her skin glow. The strapless bodice emphasized her beautiful breasts and her narrow waist.

The slightly flared skirt skimmed her hips, ending just above her knees. Maybe he had been wrong about her eyes. Now that he thought about it, her shapely legs might be her best asset.

Her smile was confident, though a bit wobbly. "You're not so bad yourself, Mr. Tarleton. Sorry I'm late. I forgot my suitcase, so we had to turn the cab around."

His gut eased. She wasn't changing her mind, thank God. "You're here now. That's all that matters."

He stood back and let Lisette introduce her friend to Mazie and J.B. Soon the judge cleared his throat, signaling his readiness to begin. Everyone took their places. Jonathan was surprised to realize that his palms were damp. It wasn't every day a man got married.

For a moment, regret speared him. This surely wasn't the scenario Lisette had imagined and anticipated as a young girl. At least he had bought her a bridal bouquet. The lilies and red roses were extravagant and over-the-top, but they lent a much-needed festive note. Lisette clutched the flowers in her left hand and slipped her right hand into his.

He blanked out after that. The occasion was surreal. Never in a million years had he imagined he'd be married in such a fashion. Not quite a shotgun wedding, but close. The judge's sonorous voice resonated in the small room. *Wilt thou take... Do you promise...* When the man in the black robe reached the part about "in sickness and in health," Lisette squeezed his fingers.

He clutched her hand, incredulous that she had agreed to his plan. He was deeply grateful for her huge heart and inherent practicality.

When it came time for the rings, he felt a sharper pinch of regret. He'd spent so many hours yesterday dealing with Tarleton Shipping business that he had completely forgotten a wedding ring. Fortunately, this morning he'd been able to rifle through the safe at the beach house and find a small signet ring that had belonged to his great-grandfather. Because the gold circlet was designed to be worn on a man's pinkie finger, the fit should work for Lisette until Jonathan could select something better.

He waited for Rebekah to relieve the bride of her bouquet. Then Jonathan took Lisette's left hand and slid the time-worn band onto the appropriate finger. *With this ring, I thee wed... With my body, I thee worship.*

The import of the ceremony slammed into him without warning, destroying everything he thought he had wanted. This was wrong. He hadn't meant to make a mockery of marriage. He'd been so focused on keeping his empire afloat he'd practically demanded Lisette's cooperation. And she'd been too kind to point out all his selfish shortcomings.

When he glanced down at her, expecting to see reproach in her gaze, her clear-eyed smile washed over him like a benediction.

The judge continued. *By the power vested in me...*

The next words penetrated the haze in Jonathan's brain and jerked him fully into the moment. "I now pronounce you husband and wife. You may kiss the bride."

He was married. Lisette Stanhope was his wife.

She looked up at him shyly, waiting. The other four adults in the room waited as well.

His body felt clumsy and uncoordinated. Jonathan Tarleton—who knew exactly what to do in any situation—was frustrated and disconcerted. Because he saw no other choice, he lowered his head and captured Lisette's mouth with his. Not the kind of erotic kiss that prompted raucous catcalls or wild applause, but a quick peck on the lips. The barest nod to convention.

When he released her, there was a split second of silence, and then everyone rushed in at once to share their congratulations.

Lisette smiled and laughed and accepted the good wishes with grace. But her gaze never met his. Not once.

It was a measure of his complete discomposure that he found his hands fisting at the sight of J.B. kissing the bride.

Then it was over. The judge had places to be. There was no wedding meal. No reception. Mazie and J.B. had offered to drop Rebekah at her condo. A hired car was waiting down below to whisk Jonathan and Lisette to the airport. Jonathan had chartered a small jet to fly them to Antigua.

Because it was far too hot to linger on the street outside, they all said their goodbyes in the lobby. Except for the large bouquet Lisette carried, there was nothing particularly festive about the moment. Rebekah and Mazie looked worried. J.B.'s gaze was guarded.

Jonathan knew they were all staring at him, trying to decide if he was going to keel over. Their unspoken concern raked his nerves and made him snappy. "We should go," he said. "The pilot will be waiting on us."

While he and J.B. retrieved Jonathan's and Lisette's luggage from the building's concierge, the women huddled together, deep in conversation.

The car was summoned. One last round of hugs. Then Jonathan found himself in the back seat of an air-conditioned sedan, seated beside his wife. *His wife.* God in heaven…

He cleared his throat. "Are you cool enough?" He adjusted the vent.

"I'm fine." Lisette's response was subdued.

They had worked in tandem for three years and had known each other much longer than that. Right now, though, she seemed like a stranger.

What was he supposed to say to her? How was he supposed to act?

Fortunately, the drive to the airport took less than half an hour. Traffic was relatively light on a Saturday afternoon.

"I think you'll enjoy the flight," he said. "No changing planes in Atlanta or Miami. Our own personal crew…two pilots and one attendant."

Lisette twisted the signet ring on her finger. "Sounds expensive."

"It's our wedding day. I thought we should splurge."

As it turned out, he was right. Lisette was visibly impressed with the plane's amenities. While the pilot finished his preflight checklist, the flight attendant—

who happened to be male—served them champagne and English biscuits.

The cookies were delicious. Jonathan didn't bother explaining that he couldn't drink the champagne. Instead, he handed his flute to Lisette when she finished hers. After a moment's hesitation, she downed the second glass. Good. If she was as nervous as he was, the Dutch courage might help.

When they were airborne, Lisette kicked off her shoes and curled her legs beneath her. She had carefully placed her wedding flowers on the empty seat beside her. Jonathan sat mere inches away, though across the small aisle.

Only the attentive presence of the flight attendant saved them from an awkward, extended silence. But after an hour that included meal service and various other polite interruptions, the flight attendant excused himself and retreated to a small cubicle at the back of the jet, leaving Jonathan and Lisette alone.

Lisette reclined her seat, reached for the small pillow and blanket and closed her eyes.

Jonathan studied her as she slept. Or maybe she was *pretending* to be asleep. Who could tell? Their honeymoon was off to a stunningly bad start. If this was how it was going to be for the next seven days, he might as well call the whole thing off.

Not that he really had that option. He and his new wife were headed to the Caribbean for a week that the outside world thought was all about sex, sex and more sex.

He snorted inwardly. He'd hoped he and Lisette could use this time to get to know each other on a more inti-

mate level, not sex *necessarily,* but he had at least en-
tertained the notion.

Even now, his body stirred at the thought of taking
his new wife to bed. At one time, it had seemed like a
possibility. Not today.

With nothing to occupy his time, he reached for the
copy of the *Wall Street Journal* that had been tucked in
the seat pocket in front of him prior to his arrival. The
usual financial predictions and analyses failed to hold
his interest for more than a few minutes.

At last he snapped the paper shut and tossed it aside,
muttering his displeasure with the newspaper in particular and the situation in general.

His travel companion stirred, sitting up and yawning. "What's the matter with you? I've traveled with
toddlers who were quieter."

"Sorry," he said, not bothering to hide his sulky tone.

She glared at him. "If you have something to say,
say it. You've been in a bad mood all afternoon. Is it
the wedding? Are you regretting what we did earlier?
Is the old ball and chain cramping your style?"

"It's everything," he said.

Ten

Lisette blinked in shock and her temper began to boil. "*You're* the one who insisted on marriage. Is the big, bad alpha wolf having second thoughts?"

His ill humor dented her feelings though she wouldn't tell him that for the world. She wasn't a real bride. If her husband chose to behave like a bear with a thorn in his paw, she shouldn't take it personally.

Jonathan stretched his arms over his head and sighed lustily. "I hate flying," he muttered.

"But you can't drive to Antigua."

"Exactly."

His scowl should have intimidated her, but she was tired of pretending this day was about love and romance. "Feel free to ignore me," she said sharply, staring out the window where white puffball clouds put on a show.

"I can't ignore you, Lizzy. That's the problem."

She spun her head so quickly her neck protested. "What does that mean?"

"You're temptation personified in that dress. I've wanted to strip it off you all afternoon."

Her jaw dropped. Heat spread from her throat to her face. "You can't be serious."

He shrugged. "I'm a man. You're my legally wed wife. No red-blooded male I know could entirely ignore the ramifications."

"I thought you were second-guessing our agreement," she whispered, her throat tight.

"I was. But not the way you're thinking. I'm frustrated that I ruined this day for you. No matter what happens next in your life, this will always be your first marriage. And as celebrations go, this one was a bust."

His wry honesty soothed some of her hurt. She waved a dismissive hand. "I wouldn't worry about it. My expectations were pretty low."

"Ouch." His shocked laugh restored her confidence. The odd balance of power between them was unprecedented territory. In their roles at Tarleton Shipping, the lines had been crisp and clear. No gray areas.

Now their entire relationship was one big gray area.

"How are you feeling?" she asked, studying his face for signs of pain or discomfort.

The scowl returned, though not as dark and brooding as before. "I don't want to talk about my health, remember?"

"So I'm never allowed to check on my husband's welfare? That seems cold. I'd do the same for an acquaintance who was ill."

"I'm not ill," he snapped.

"I don't understand."

He unfastened his seat belt and stood up to walk the aisle. Back and forth. His energy and passion, momentarily chained by circumstances, nevertheless vibrated in the close confines of the jet's cabin.

Without warning, the plane jolted and Jonathan staggered.

The attendant stuck his head out at the back of the plane, intercom phone in hand. "Rough weather up ahead, sir. You'll have to take your seat."

Jonathan nodded and sat down, belting in with quick, practiced movements. He glanced at Lisette. "You okay?"

"I'm fine. You never answered my question."

"It wasn't really a question as I recall."

"Don't play with words. Why did you say you aren't ill?"

He stared straight ahead, his classic male profile carved in grim lines. At last he exhaled. "I have a time bomb inside my skull. But I won't tiptoe around, always worrying about when and if it's going to blow up and kill me. I have a life to live. A future to plan, though it might not be as long as I had hoped. I'm not going to spend every waking day assessing my slow decay. I can't do that. I won't. Do you understand?"

His hands gripped the armrests so tightly his knuckles turned white. She knew he wasn't afraid to fly, so his turmoil came from another source.

Lisette reached out her right hand and linked her fingers with his. "I do," she said quietly. "I won't ask again, or at least I'll try not to. As far as I'm concerned, you're going to live until you're ninety. Does that work for you?"

Some of his tension winnowed away. He shot her a

sideways glance that was both sheepish and relieved. "Thanks." His thumb caressed the back of her hand. "I swear I'll ask for help when the time comes."

"Fair enough." She hadn't realized that holding hands with her husband on her wedding day was going to affect her so strongly. She had reached out to him in a gesture of comfort and understanding. Now she was reluctant to let go. But she did. She was a wife in name only.

Gradually the turbulence outside the plane subsided. The flight attendant reappeared with coffee and sodas and snacks. "We'll be on the ground in forty-five minutes," he said.

"So soon?" She was startled.

Jonathan's smile was smug. "And now you know the benefits of chartering a private jet. Hassle-free. Besides, nothing is too good for my new bride."

The flight attendant smiled, so their charade must be working. Maybe no one would be able to tell they weren't really a couple.

Landing in St. John's and deplaning was smooth and easy. Jonathan had planned this end of the trip as well. Instead of a private car, he had arranged to rent a four-wheel-drive vehicle that would handle the sometimes precipitous roads leading up to his friend's hillside villa just below Shirley Heights.

The air was lush and humid, but not more so than Charleston, and the wind off the ocean was heavenly. Flowering trees and shrubs scented the air with exotic fragrances.

After loading their things into the back of the Jeep, Jonathan helped her up into the high passenger seat, and soon they were off on the next leg of their journey. He handled the narrow, rough road with confidence. When they pulled up in front of the beautiful home that was to be their own private retreat for the week, Lisette was speechless. She wasn't sure what she had expected, but it wasn't this lavish, stunning luxury.

A uniformed maid met them and gave them a brief tour before excusing herself to finish preparing their dinner. The house overlooked English Harbour, a glittering field of blue dotted with a hundred sailboats. Colorful bougainvillea surrounded the property and draped over railings.

"We can have dinner here," Jonathan said, indicating the elegant glass-and-rattan table on the wide veranda. "A bird's-eye view for our first sunset."

"That sounds perfect."

His gaze raked her from head to toe. "You look beautiful in that dress, but would you like to change into something more comfortable for the rest of the evening?"

She searched his words for hidden meanings, but found none. The thought of a cool shower after a busy day of wedding preparations and travel sounded wonderful.

"I would," she said. "If it's just us, we don't have to be formal, do we?"

"Not at all. This week is ours."

His quiet words and the intimacy in his smile sent a thrill through her body. Spending time with Jonathan under any circumstance would be enjoyable. He was a charismatic, fascinating man. But he was also intensely virile and masculine, and she dared not let herself think about what might unfold here in this tropical paradise.

The maid had shown them the master suite with its

hedonistic glass-walled shower. Jonathan fetched both large suitcases from the Jeep and placed them on matching teak chests at the foot of the massive king-size bed. Its carved posts reflected the English colonial influence in Antigua, as did the vibrantly colored watercolors depicting points of historical interest, which were spread around the room.

Lisette set their carry-ons beside the dresser. Being here with Jonathan in this lovely room that was so obviously created for couples to enjoy rattled her considerably. "I'll use the bathroom across the hall," she said, trying not to look at either the bed *or* her new husband. "We don't want to be late for our first meal. The maid said half an hour." She grabbed what she needed and tried to smile as if her nerves weren't escalating by the minute.

Jonathan nodded, his gaze hooded. "Sounds good."

She clutched her toiletry kit and clothes and fled. In the other room she locked the door and collapsed onto the bed, her heart pounding in her chest. Did Jonathan mean for them to be intimate tonight?

The prospect filled her with a confusing mixture of anticipation and dread. The sexual attraction between them was no longer veiled. Jonathan didn't even try to hide the hunger in his gaze. But he had said they needed time to get used to each other. Was that only for her benefit?

Probably. Men rarely missed a chance to be physically intimate with a woman when the woman was available and interested.

As his wife, she was definitely available. And she had been interested for a long time.

Though she needed breathing space to find her bearings, the clock was not her friend. She undressed and jumped in the shower, keeping the water frigid. The brisk jolt of cold against her heated flesh revived and refreshed her. Wrapping up in a thick terry robe afterward felt wonderful.

She had worn her hair up in a complicated knot for the wedding and the flight. Now she took it down and brushed it out. Carefully she caught back the sides in gold clips and stared at herself in the mirror.

Jonathan claimed he'd had no serious relationships recently. She had no reason to doubt him. Even so, the prospect of getting naked with him was intimidating. Her own sexual experience was fairly limited, and she certainly couldn't match his innate confidence.

Nevertheless, she had made a monumental decision on her own behalf. After being halfway in love with her handsome boss for a very long time, now they were alone together, sharing a faux honeymoon. If the moment seemed right and Jonathan was receptive, she was going to let him know she wanted a real marriage in every sense of the word. And she was going to revisit the baby idea whether he liked it or not. She was giving up a lot for him.

Sighing deeply, she picked up the outfit she had chosen for this first evening. The garment was loose and flowing, with a halter neck. What made the dress provocative was the partially sheer lawn fabric. The color was ecru, adding to the impression that she was seminude. Tiny gold threads sifted through the cotton from throat to toe, catching the light with each movement.

She dropped the robe to the floor and debated the available undergarments. Dispensing with her bra wasn't a hard choice. She slid the lovely dress over her head and let it fall to her bare feet. The incredibly soft material caressed her sensitive skin. Though her rigid nipples pressed against the cloth in a provocative fashion, the look was certainly appropriate for an intimate dinner, particularly during a honeymoon.

The impulse to go full commando was strong, but she wasn't quite that brave. So she stepped into the brand-new pair of undies she had bought yesterday afternoon at a lingerie boutique. The lacy thong matched the color of her skin and did nothing to disturb the pleasing flow of the dress.

Her light eye makeup still looked good, though she added a bit of dramatic color for the evening. Then, all that was left was to add some gloss to her lips.

When she was ready, she stepped back and tried to study her reflection as a man would. The dress flattered her body and hinted at more curves beneath.

Would her new husband like the way she looked?

Her heart rapped in her chest as if she had run a mile. She tried to take a deep breath, but it didn't help.

She was nervous as a skittish Victorian virgin on her wedding night.

When she could delay no longer, she opened the guest room door and peeked out into the hall. Jonathan had left the master suite open, so she was able to see that the room was empty. Unless he was still in the bathroom, which seemed doubtful.

She had spent far too long getting ready. Jonathan was probably on the terrace waiting for her.

Her instincts were correct. She found him standing at the low stone wall, staring out at the idyllic scene below as if he hadn't a care in the world. His appearance surprised her. Instead of his customary dark suit and tie, he wore lightweight khaki pants and a crisp white linen shirt that stretched across broad shoulders. Leather deck shoes with no socks completed the look of a man on vacation.

For some reason, this relaxed version of Jonathan made him seem like a stranger.

She inhaled sharply. "I hope dinner is ready. I'm starving."

Jonathan spun around. All the blood in his body rushed to his groin in a painful arousal that left him unsteady on his feet. "Lizzy," he muttered. "You're here." Her tentative smile dazzled him. Why had he ever thought of her as average? Now that they were on intimate terms, her subtle, understated beauty caught him by the throat and wouldn't let go.

She was wearing some kind of sultry dress that was designed to make a man drool and stutter. It clung to her stellar breasts and slid over her body like a raw caress. Was she naked underneath? The possibility consumed him.

The maid appeared at exactly the wrong time. Jonathan wanted to curse at her and send her away, but the tray she carried was laden with culinary delights that made his stomach rumble even in the midst of his desperate desire for his bride.

The table was situated so that both parties had an unobstructed view of the ocean. He held Lizzy's chair and waited for her to be seated. Her hair brushed her bare shoulders. He wanted to run his fingers through it.

Instead, he took his place across from her and listened with half an ear as the maid/cook explained each dish. There were fried plantains and local grouper with pineapple chutney. Toast points with a Creole dipping sauce and a beautiful key lime pie.

Lisette chatted animatedly with the older local woman, at last coaxing a smile from her dour, expressionless face. Jonathan was struck suddenly by how different he and Lizzy were in temperament. She opened herself up to everyone, while Jonathan kept himself in check.

His recent diagnosis had only exacerbated his instinct to hide behind his CEO persona. Even so—sweet, generous, compassionate Lisette had agreed to his outlandish plan. Perhaps unconsciously, he had known she would. Which made him an opportunist and a user.

The realization shamed him, because it was too late for second thoughts.

Once the maid was assured that Jonathan and Lisette had everything they needed, she disappeared, leaving the newlyweds to their private wedding-night feast.

Jonathan forced himself to eat and talk and smile. Everything a normal groom would do. Some of his turmoil subsided, winnowed away by the sheer magic of a tropical night.

Lisette leaned back in her chair, meal forgotten, when the sun neared the horizon. "I can't imagine this would ever get old," she whispered. She reached across the table and took his hand. "Watch it with me," she said. "And make a wish."

He gripped her fingers, feeling how slender and delicate they were in contrast to his larger hand. "I don't think that's a real thing. Isn't it only shooting stars?"

"It can be whatever we want it to be. Look," she said urgently. The sun seemed to sink more quickly now.

The bottom rim kissed the ocean. The sun melted into a fatter, wider ball, and then it was gone.

Jonathan stared at the colors swirling on the horizon. How many more sunsets would he live to see?

He cleared his throat. "I understand now why my buddy bought this place. It's more than a tax write-off."

Lisette grimaced. "A tax write-off? Oh, Jonathan. Surely you have a tiny bit of romance in your soul."

"Maybe. Did you make a wish?"

"I did, but I'm not telling you."

"I'll bet I could make you talk."

She blinked, perhaps as surprised as he was by the blatantly sexual comment. He hadn't even known he was going to say it.

"Um…" She released his hand. "May I ask you something?"

He waved a hand. "I'm feeling pretty mellow at the moment. The floor is yours, my beautiful bride."

"We've danced around the issue of whether or not this marriage, *our* marriage, is going to include physical intimacy. And we talked about having time to get used to each other…to know each other in a different way than we do at work."

Her pause was so long he felt compelled to say something. "Yes."

"You said it would be up to me."

"Yes." The word was more of a croak.

"Well…" She hesitated. Though he couldn't be sure with only candlelight to illuminate her face, he thought she had blushed. "Waiting for the shoe to drop makes me nervous and jumpy around you. I think I'd rather go ahead and get it over with. If you don't mind."

Eleven

He scowled. "Like a root canal or tetanus shot? Pardon me if I'm not flattered." In fact, he was downright insulted. No woman had ever approached sex with him as a hurdle to be overcome. "I told you, our marriage doesn't have to include physical intimacy at all."

"That came out wrong. This is my first wedding night, and I don't have a script."

"I haven't ever been married either, but I'm pretty damned sure a real husband and wife would have had sex *before* dinner. Or maybe skipped dinner altogether." He was practically shouting at her and he didn't know why. Except that he wanted to slide that tantalizing dress from her body and see what Lisette Stanhope would be like in bed.

"I'm sorry," she said, the words stiff. "I didn't mean to make you angry. Forget I said anything."

He stood abruptly. Arousal coursed through his veins, pulsating and urgent. If he didn't get some space—some breathing room—he was going to take her right here on the dinner table. "Excuse me," he muttered.

"Don't you want dessert?"

"Screw dessert," he snarled.

An hour later, Lisette sat with her bare feet propped on the railing and toyed with a piece of key lime pie. It was actually one of her favorites, and this particular version was the best she had ever tasted. But her stomach was tied in knots.

The maid had cleared the table not long after Jonathan's stormy exit. A short while later the silent woman climbed into her car for the trip home. Lisette had heard the steady chug of the old engine as it made its way down the mountain.

She replayed the evening in her head, wondering how she might have approached things differently. She hadn't expected problems to crop up so soon. It looked like the honeymoon period was over. She couldn't even laugh at her own joke.

The sky was dark now, punctuated with a million stars. The night wasn't quiet. Birds and other unseen animals spoke to each other in interesting choruses. Because she had napped on the plane, she wasn't sleepy at all. It was far more entertaining to stay out here and absorb the Caribbean magic than it would be to toss and turn in an unfamiliar bed.

Besides, she couldn't share a bed with Jonathan. Not now. Had he put her suitcase in the guest room? Or moved his own? She was too much of a chicken to go inside and find out.

She had to get through six days and six more nights of this before they could go home. The villa had a jewel of a swimming pool, and she had brought two brand-new swimsuits. Maybe she could read and work on the summer tan she never seemed to manage.

Tears of regret stung her eyes, but she refused to let them fall. Jonathan's rejection of her awkward overture had hurt. It still hurt.

All she'd been trying to tell him was that she was ready. She wanted him. Instead, she had made it sound like sleeping with her new husband was a chore and an obligation. No wonder he lost his cool.

She set the small china plate with the pie crumbs on the wall and leaned back so she could see more of the sky. Never had she been more confused or more unsure of herself. Helping Jonathan through these next weeks and months was something she *wanted* to do…something she needed to do.

He was a decent, kind, hardworking man who had been dealt an abominably bad hand. He was also exactly the kind of man she had always looked for in a life partner. But none had ever come along until Jonathan. Or at least not one who made her body quiver with desire. She wanted him. Desperately.

What did *she* know about seduction? Apparently nothing. She and Jonathan were married and planted smack-dab in the midst of a tropical paradise, and yet still she had bobbled it. She hadn't wanted to be a passive female, waiting for him to make the first move. She'd wanted to assert her femininity, to be bold and fearless.

Maybe men didn't like that in a woman. Maybe they

always wanted to be the aggressor. At least in the beginning.

It was late. She should probably go in.

Before she could follow through on that thought, a deep male voice sounded behind her.

"Lisette…"

That was all. Just her name.

She stood up and faced him. "Yes?"

He shrugged. "I'm sorry."

"I'm sorry, too."

Without saying another word, he took his phone from his pocket, tapped a few icons and set the device on the table. A slow, sultry cascade of music filled the air. Jonathan held out his hand. "Will you dance with me?"

Never in a million years would she have pegged Jonathan Tarleton for a dancer, but he proved her wrong. He was both light on his feet and moved with natural rhythm. As he swept her into his arms and twirled them across the flagstone patio, it seemed as if they were dancing on clouds.

With her cheek pressed to his chest, she noted his ragged breathing, his thudding pulse. He held her tightly, close enough for him to know that she was essentially naked beneath her dress. They danced in bare feet. The differences in their heights made her feel cherished and protected.

One song ended. Another began. She couldn't ignore the way his aroused sex pressed against her abdomen.

She didn't know what to say, but there was no real need for conversation. Their bodies communicated without words.

After a few more songs, the music ended. Before she could do more than inhale a shocked breath, she felt

Jonathan's fingers play with the knot at her nape. "May I?" he asked, his breath warm on her ear.

A hard shiver rocked through her body. "Yes."

Moments later, with a gentle tug from him, her dress fell in a pool at her feet. He took a step back and stared. "I want a do-over," he said hoarsely.

She wrapped her arms around her breasts, equal parts excited and uncertain. "Me, too. I want to sleep with you, Jonathan. Very much."

He raised an eyebrow. "Sleep?"

"Don't tease me. Not now. I'm trying to play this cool and sophisticated. But I'm at a definite disadvantage."

Her wry comment coaxed a grin from him. "What if I take off my shirt?" He tackled the buttons so fast she laughed out loud. But when his chest was bare, her levity dried up.

She cocked her head. "If I had known you were hiding a six-pack beneath those hand-tailored suits," she said, "I would have hit on you a long time ago."

He scooped her up in his arms, his gaze hot and hungry. "No, you wouldn't. You've always been the consummate professional. You never even hinted that you were interested in me."

"Of course not," she whispered. "You were my boss."

He kicked open the door, carried her into the house and bumped the door shut with his hip before locking it. "And now I'm your husband."

"Yes, you are." She cupped his cheek with her hand. "I'm glad you changed your mind. I'm sorry I made sex with you sound like something I was tolerating. I didn't want to wait, but my words came out all wrong."

"I'll let you make it up to me." He strode in the direction of the bedroom. In the doorway, he paused. "I have a confession." He dropped her onto the mattress and settled beside her, placing one hand, palm flat, on her stomach. His dark eyes glittered. "I'm very much afraid I came up with the marriage idea because I was obsessed with you…not because I cared about Tarleton Shipping."

Being mostly naked with Jonathan in a huge, hedonistic bed should have embarrassed her, but all she could think about was how very much she wanted him. "Maybe it was both," she said. "I'm okay with that."

He stood up and stripped off his pants and boxers. The sight of his aroused sex dried her mouth. His body was intensely masculine and incredibly beautiful. For a man who purportedly worked long hours, he surely did *something* to maintain that physique.

When he reached into his pants pocket for a trio of condoms, she realized that the reason he had come out to the terrace to make peace was because he wanted more than a platonic wedding night.

His crooked smile found its way into her heart and made her eyes sting with emotional tears. She loved him. It was the only reason she had said yes to this inconvenient marriage.

She still wanted a baby, but since they had come close to ruining this first night, she wouldn't bring it up. Yet…

She flipped back the covers and held out her hand. "Come get warm." The tile floor was icy with the AC running.

Though the bed was large, when Jonathan joined her, his big, masculine body dominated the space. She tried to scoot farther to one side, but he grabbed her wrist. "Come here, Ms. Tarleton." Leaning over her on one elbow, he brushed the hair from her face. "I want a real honeymoon," he said softly. The words were not particularly provocative, but the expression on his face made her tremble.

She touched his shoulder, stroking the hard planes where smooth, taut skin stretched over muscle and bone. "So do I."

He let her explore for several long moments, not moving at all. But the flush on his cheekbones darkened. "I like having you touch me, Lizzy."

When he cupped her breast and teased her nipple with his thumb, she gasped. Heat bloomed and streaked through her body like an erotic pinball, flipping switches she didn't even know existed.

She tried to say something, but he bent his head and tasted the furled flesh, raking it with his teeth. Her hands clenched in his hair as all the breath wheezed out of her lungs.

It was almost laughable to think about how she had imagined this moment. In her mind, the first time with Jonathan was going to be tender and gentle. Why she'd held that notion, she couldn't say.

The reality was totally unlike her fantasies. It was far more visceral, more powerful. He staked his claim without apology.

He touched her everywhere.

And all along the way, he muttered praises and pleas and demands. He allowed her neither timidity nor inhibitions. His hunger ignited her own, taking her to places she hadn't experienced.

They tumbled across the mattress, wrestling for the upper hand, both determined to drive the other to the edge. Jonathan dragged her lacy undies down her legs, careful not to tear them. She wouldn't have minded.

Now he moved lower in the bed. "I want to taste you," he said. "Spread your legs." Three words. Three little words, and she was his slave.

His intimate demand shocked her. For a moment, her thighs tightened instinctively.

As he moved to his elbows and nudged her ankles apart, he lifted his head, staring at her challengingly. "Too much, Lizzy?"

She forced herself to relax. "No," she said softly. "Never."

Jonathan was skilled at more than dancing. He shot her over the edge of her first climax with dizzying speed. Her body was his. He played it like a master, demanding her total submission to his will.

Though she wanted to give him the same pleasure he was giving her, she barely had time to breathe or choke out a cry of completion. He gave no quarter, drawing out the incredible bliss of orgasm until she was weak and spent.

At last he let her rest. "You're amazing," he said, resting his cheek on her upper thigh. "Maybe we'll never leave this room."

With his hair tumbled across his forehead and his pupils dilated with arousal, he looked very different from the man who controlled a huge business empire with cool confidence. Tonight he was naked and voracious, utterly male, completely devoted to pleasing his bride.

She still trembled from their recent excess. "I've waited a long time for this," she said. The words were only slightly unsteady. "I want you on your back, Jonathan, so I can have my way with you."

The muscles in his throat rippled as he swallowed. His erection bumped her knee. "Should I be scared?" he joked as he rolled away from her and sprawled on the empty side of the bed.

"Very."

He tucked his hands behind his head. His cocky grin made him look young and carefree. For a moment, her heart wrestled with the reality of the future, but she shoved the bad thoughts aside. No time for tears or mourning now.

Despite what had just happened, she was shy about him seeing her naked. While she debated how best to play with him, she wrapped the coverlet from the foot of the bed around herself and clutched it with one hand.

Her gaze landed on a beautiful azure-glazed urn filled with dry grasses. She plucked one out of the container and brushed the fluffy tip against her arm. "This will do," she said.

Jonathan's eyes widened. Perhaps he had been expecting oral sex. Everything in its time. She wanted to keep her new husband off balance. He leaned toward arrogance at times. It wouldn't be a bad thing for him to wonder what she was up to.

Trying to climb back onto the bed without losing either her weapon of torment *or* her covering was virtually impossible.

Jonathan smirked. "I've seen all there is to see. No reason to be shy with me now."

The challenge in his voice tipped her decision. She dropped the soft throw and stood at the side of the bed, naked and in charge. Or at least that's what she was shooting for. Jonathan's searing gaze, intense and bold, was almost enough to melt her into a puddle.

"I'm not shy," she lied. "I was merely planning my assault."

"Sounds dangerous."

She ran her hand down his thigh, carefully avoiding the interesting territory nearby. "Close your eyes, Jonathan. Relax."

He obeyed the first command, but choked out an incredulous laugh. "Relax? You can't be serious. You've got me so tightly wound I might go up in flames."

"I have faith in you," she said, leaning down to kiss his sculpted lips. She let the tip of her tongue push inside his mouth and brush *his* tongue. "Whatever you do, don't open your eyes. Just glide on a sea of pleasure. One muscle at a time." She lowered her voice to a murmur. "I want you to feel *everything*. Do you understand?"

He nodded, his jaw tight. "I'll try."

With the feathery end of her long frond, she started at his ears and his cheeks, caressing one at a time. He gasped once, sharply, and his hands fisted at his hips. Slowly she moved the seagrass along his sternum and over his belly. When she neared his erection, his entire body went rigid and a ragged moan escaped him. "Not yet," she murmured. "You're too tense. You want to be in control, don't you, Jonathan?"

"Hell, yes."

She slid the fluffy tip across the tops of his thighs, *accidentally* brushing his vulnerable sac in the process. Then it was on to his calves, his ankles and his big, unabashedly male feet.

"Letting go can be wonderful," she promised.

The word he said made her smile. He was clearly trying to indulge her and so very clearly losing the battle.

Now she hovered the stalk of seagrass over his body and let the soft tip toy with his erection. His sex was swollen and hard, flat against his belly. Importunate. Ready for action.

When she touched him like that, a giant shudder racked his frame. "Please," he muttered. "No more."

She dropped the dried plant and climbed onto the bed, taking his sex in her hands and squeezing gently.

Before she could taste him intimately, his control snapped. He reared up and took her head in his two hands, dragging her mouth to his, kissing her desperately. "I can't wait," he groaned. "Now, Lizzy. Now."

He reached blindly for one of the condoms. A fleeting regret swept through her. Would he ever change his mind about the baby?

But then he was on top of her and in her and her world exploded. When she grabbed his shoulders, her nails sank into his flesh. He grunted in pain, but didn't stop. She didn't want him to. Ever. The feel of his body taking hers would be imprinted in her memory forever.

Canting her hips, she urged him deeper and deeper still until the blunt head of his sex pressed her womb. "Jonathan…" she cried out. Suddenly she was both elated and terrified. She would never be able to protect her heart. Not if things were like this between them.

There was no room for subterfuge, no opportunity for self-defense.

"Relax, Lizzy." It was his turn to say the word. He must have felt her moment of indecision. His lips nuzzled her ear. "I want you every way there is to want a woman," he said. His voice was rough, almost inaudible. "You're mine," he said. "For as long as we have."

Even the fact that he brought reality into their bed

couldn't stop the headlong rush into abandon. "Yes," she moaned. "Yes."

Stunned fulfillment caught her yet again and swept her into the currents of his passion. Jonathan went rigid and thrust inside her forever, it seemed, until he found his own release and collapsed on top of her.

Twelve

God in heaven. What have we done? Jonathan was groggy and satiated. His limbs were numb, his brain fogged with a jumble of thoughts that didn't quite coalesce into reason.

When he could open one eye, he determined that his new wife slept…draped over him like a soft, curvy boa. And that vision, only that, was enough to have his sex stirring again.

If he had known it would be like this, he might never have been able to leave her alone for these last three years. Tonight had shown him a whole new side of Lisette Stanhope. She was strong and capable. He knew that much, of course. But she was also sexually adventurous and fun in bed.

She'd been hiding behind sensible skirts and tops and boring colors. Here, in Antigua, her sexuality had blossomed. Or maybe it had been there along, and she had simply kept it from him.

Suddenly an unpleasant thought occurred. His new bride wasn't a virgin. He knew that, of course. She was thirty-seven years old. But where had she learned how to turn a man into a drooling idiot? Jonathan liked being able to drive *her* wild, but when she turned the tables on him and used a pseudomassage to push him to the edge of his control, the experience was less comfortable.

Incredibly arousing and erotically eye-opening, but still a disturbing moment. He'd never had sex like that with *any* woman. Not that the mechanics were so very different. But it was the mood, the way his body responded as if his arousal and his sexual response had been conditioned by the scent of her skin and the sound of her voice.

He slid out of bed and visited the facilities. Lisette was still deeply asleep, so he grabbed a quick shower. When he walked back into the bedroom—towel tied at his hips—her eyes were open.

She lifted up on her elbows. The sheet slithered below her breasts. His towel tented in the front. "Good morning," she said huskily.

"Good morning to you." He couldn't do a thing in the world about the lewdly fashioned terry cloth at his groin.

Lisette pretended not to notice. "Does the maid come first thing?"

"I was told there would be plenty of food in the fridge for breakfast and lunch. Sunday is her day off. We're all alone."

Those incredible pale green eyes studied him intently. "Is that information I need to know?"

It was impossible to miss the challenge in her gaze. He nodded slowly. "I didn't want you to worry."

"Worry?"

"You know. About being interrupted. This bedroom is entirely private. Off-limits."

"Ah."

He sat down on the edge of the mattress. "Did you sleep well?"

"I must have. I don't really recall last night. I think I was dead to the world."

"That's a shame. Parts of it were pretty damned spectacular."

Her lips twitched. "Oh, *that* part. Yeah. I remember that."

He ditched the towel and reached for her. "How hungry are you on a scale of one to ten?" Lifting her on top of him, he stroked her bottom.

Her chest heaved in a sigh. "I had my heart set on an omelet, but an appetizer might be nice."

He took a moment to enjoy the view. With her hair tousled and her pale skin warm from their bed, just looking at her gave him an odd ache in his chest. She was easier with him now, less tentative. Last night had cemented something in their relationship.

"At the risk of sounding like a sex-obsessed male," he said, "I have to tell you your breasts are spectacular." Firm, smooth flesh. Raspberry tips. A sudden vision of his wife nursing their child flashed into his mind. He knew Lisette wanted a baby. She had made that very clear. The prospect of trying to get her pregnant fried his brain. It was too soon to make a decision like that, but suddenly, it wasn't out of the question.

"Be honest," he said, breathing heavily. "You wore that dress last night to drive me insane."

"It was a hot evening." Her smile was innocent.

He snorted. "It's hot in Charleston, but I've never seen you in anything remotely similar."

"You only see me at work. Maybe I dress like that all the time when I'm out on the town."

He pulled her down for a quick kiss. "Do you?"

"No."

Lisette realized that things were escalating rapidly. Unfortunately, she badly needed to visit the bathroom and freshen up. "Jonathan?"

"Hmm?" He nibbled the side of her neck, just below her right ear.

She shuddered. "Give me three minutes," she said, scrambling off her provocative perch and fleeing. In the bathroom, she closed the door, hoping he didn't hear the quiet snick of the lock. She needed privacy, but more than that, she needed a moment to steady her thoughts, to find solid ground.

After taking care of urgent needs, she did a few quick ablutions, then leaned forward on the vanity and studied her face in the mirror. She was a married woman now. A legal part of Jonathan's life. Whatever faced them, she would be with him day after day. His wife, for better or worse.

When she had awakened a little while ago and spotted him standing in the doorway, he almost seemed like a stranger. In all the years she had known him, never once had she seen him unshaven. Today, dark stubble shadowed his firm jaw, giving him a rakish air. The change was unexpected, but she definitely liked it. Scruffy Jonathan was even more appealing than tuxedo-clad Jonathan.

She returned to the bedroom with a mix of anticipation and trepidation. Daylight sex was different. Harder for a woman to hide an extra five pounds or pretend to be a seductress when in reality she was anything but.

Jonathan was looking at his phone, but he tossed it aside as soon as she appeared. His smile made her toes curl against the cool tile. "Hey," he said, his greeting warm and husky. "Come join me."

Though she felt shy even now, he didn't have to ask her twice. She chewed her bottom lip, trying not to notice the way her stomach flipped and went into free fall when Jonathan pulled her close and stroked her arm. Her *arm*, for Pete's sake. When he eventually moved to other body parts, she would be a goner.

She cleared her throat. "What would you like to do today?" she asked, wincing inwardly at hearing herself. She sounded like a perky travel agent.

Her husband's low chuckle didn't help her embarrassment. "You mean after sex and breakfast? At the rate we're going, there won't be much of the day left."

"Are you complaining?" She laid her hand on his hair-roughened upper thigh, feeling the taut muscles.

"Lord, no. I'm even willing to give up breakfast if my wife keeps me busy all morning."

As if on cue, Lisette's stomach growled. She curled into his side, putting her hand, palm flat, right over his heart. One of her legs trapped both of his, but there was no question as to who was in control.

He shifted without warning and put her beneath him, kissing her lazily. His lips were firm and persuasive.

"How hungry *are* you?" he asked, nuzzling her nose with his.

Feelings rose in her chest, wild poignant emotions that choked her, making it hard to breathe. How was she supposed to be blasé about this? Most normal honeymooners would be planning their future. Instead, Jonathan was asking her to live only in the moment. It was far harder than she had thought it would be to pretend.

She managed a smile. "Hungry for you," she said lightly. "The other can wait."

Maybe Jonathan sensed her ambivalence, because after reaching for protection, he stroked her body so carefully and so gently she nearly cried for real this time. How was she going to protect herself? Being with him like this was too real, too devastatingly sweet. The thought of losing him was more than she could bear.

He entered her slowly, so slowly she was forced to wrap her ankles behind his back and urge him deeper. The more she tried, the more he taunted them both.

His voice was rough, unsteady. "Tell me how you like it, beautiful girl. Slow and infinite? Or hard and fast? I'll give you whatever you ask."

Her good intentions cracked. "Give me a baby, Jonathan. Please." The words slipped out of their own volition, born of a need to keep part of him with her forever. As soon as she spoke, she knew she had ruined the magic.

Jonathan was close to the edge, but he rolled away, grim-faced, and disappeared into the bathroom.

Tears wet her cheeks as she grabbed her things and sought the relative safety of the guest room. She couldn't do this. It wasn't fair.

She buried her face in the pillows that didn't carry

his scent and cried until her chest hurt and her eyes were puffy. They had barely made it twenty-four hours, and already their marriage was on the rocks.

He was asking the impossible. *Be his stand-in at work. His bed partner at home.* But don't love. Don't try to make any of this real.

This relationship wasn't working out as she had planned. She thought she could be satisfied with having a small bit of his life. That she could let him go when the time came.

But now, she wasn't at all sure she would be able to play her part. It was too damn hard.

At last she rose and showered. Afterward she put on one of her new bikinis and topped it with a modest cover-up. When hunger drove her to the kitchen, she found evidence that her husband had dined earlier. For her part, a banana and yogurt with granola were all that she could manage…that, and hot black coffee with plenty of sugar.

Unlike yesterday evening, today there were no mutual apologies in the hours that followed. No dancing on the terrace.

Lisette swam and sunbathed. Jonathan appeared eventually and claimed a lounger at the opposite end of the pool. He buried his face in a business magazine and occasionally slept.

What he did *not* do was make any attempt to converse at all.

She was hurt and angry, but she wouldn't apologize for feeling the way she did. It wasn't unreasonable of her to ask for a baby, or even to demand one. She was giving up her dreams for Jonathan. He had promised to consider the pregnancy. Had he not really meant it?

Perhaps there was a better way to smooth over their mutual wounds. Something very basic and elemental like the need between a man and a woman.

When the heat from the late-afternoon sun became intense, she removed her cover-up and applied more sunscreen. With her back to Jonathan, she twisted her hair into a messy knot and then bent over to pick up the brush she had intentionally dropped. Was he watching? She had never done anything so physically manipulative in her life, but desperate times and all that.

Instead of using the diving board as she had earlier, she donned her sunglasses and entered the water via the shallow steps…which just happened to be on *Jonathan's* end of the pool. After that, she did lazy laps, one after the other. On each return trip, she peeked at her companion. Hiding behind her darkened lenses allowed her to observe him without his being entirely sure that she was.

He definitely wasn't sleeping any longer.

His board shorts meant she couldn't tell if he was responding physically to her deliberate teasing, but at last she noticed that his hands clenched the arms of the lounger.

Bingo… He couldn't ignore her. That was what she was counting on. They might not have everything going for them that a normal couple would, but there was plenty of room for progress.

Jonathan couldn't stonewall her about this baby thing. He wanted her too badly, and she felt the same way about him.

Righteous indignation and lust were a dangerous combination. Jonathan was not happy with how things had unfolded today, but he refused to go crawling to his bride. She understood how he felt. He'd made his position very clear.

He was a master negotiator, and he knew from experience that it was always better to make an adversary come to him, not vice versa.

So he stayed where he was and told himself he was in the right.

Which was cold comfort when Lisette stood up in the shallow end and sluiced water from her curvy body with both hands.

By Caribbean standards, her navy bikini was probably puritanical, but damn it, her breasts were about to pop out of that top. And as for the bottom half, well, he couldn't get his mind off the gorgeous erotic secrets that were his for the taking, barely covered. Wet and warm. Perfectly feminine.

When she turned her back on him for the hundredth time, it seemed, and swam lazily toward the other end of the pool, he'd had enough. He lunged to his feet, strode down the steps and bulleted toward his prey as silently as a shark. He'd been on the varsity swim team in college, and he had lived at the shore his entire life.

Lisette Stanhope Tarleton didn't have a chance.

A heartbeat later, he glided up beneath her and wrapped his arms around her legs, dragging her under. The water at this end was deep. The sudden move knocked her sunglasses loose. Her wide-eyed gaze met his under the water. Sunlight showered down on them through the ripples in the pool.

He put his hand behind her neck and pulled her close for a hard kiss. Then he kicked hard and shot them both back to the surface. When they could breathe, he put his hands at her waist and lifted her as high as he could. "Grab the diving board, Lizzy."

She obeyed, but her face mirrored her confusion. "What are we doing? Some kind of kinky yoga?"

"Call it whatever you want, Ms. Tarleton. But don't let go." Lazily, as if every nerve in his body wasn't scraped raw by the lust pounding in his limbs, he reached out and dragged her bikini top below her breasts.

It was a dicey game he played. Staying afloat required him to move his legs continually. He curled an arm around her waist. That was better. Now he could take one berry-colored nipple into his mouth without drowning.

Her skin tasted of chlorine and coconut oil. He might as well have been tasting her sex, so visceral was his reaction. With his free hand, he tugged the bottom half of her suit to her ankles, freed it completely and tossed it up on the side of the pool. The bikini top followed. Gently he entered her with two fingers. Her inner muscles tightened.

"Jonathan?" The single word was breathless.

"I don't know what to do with you," he muttered, stunned enough by his own weakness to be completely honest.

"We could try the shallow end."

It took him half a second to realize that while he was pondering the greater questions of life, Lisette had taken his comment at face value and was offering a practical solution.

"Yes, we could," he said. "You can let go now, sweetheart. I've got you." He tugged her through the water to the center of the pool where the water was neck deep.

Her arms were still linked around his shoulders, even though she no longer needed his support.

Her eyelashes were spiky and wet. Her almost translucent green eyes stared deep into his soul. Or that's how it seemed for a hushed moment.

She rubbed a drop of water from his chin. "I like this pirate look," she said softly. "Too bad he has to disappear when we go home."

"Being the boss does occasionally have its downside." He kissed her nose and her bare, pink lips. "I want to take you right here. Just like this." The notion consumed him.

A shadow danced across her face. "No condoms, remember?"

"I won't come inside you."

She shook her head slowly. "I can't take that chance. Not when you're so adamant about not having a baby. I want you to make me pregnant, but it has to be a conscious choice on your part."

Damn it. Nothing like having a lover throw your own words back at you. "Put your legs around me," he coaxed. Lisette was blissfully naked, but Jonathan was still wearing his swim trunks. Nothing could happen.

The water made her buoyant. She granted his request easily. Now her breasts were snuggled into his chest and those long, gorgeous legs wrapped tightly around his waist.

She nibbled his earlobe. "We have a wonderful, comfy bed inside. I bet we could get there if we tried."

His body quaked. He rubbed his hardened sex against her center, tormenting them both. Lisette buried her face in his shoulder and moaned.

"I want you," he said, the words hoarse and raspy.

For a mad moment, he almost caved. Making Lisette pregnant was a titillating idea, one that messed with his head. He could do it. Right now. Give her a baby. His child.

But his will was stronger than his desire. Because he cared about her. Being a single parent was hard and lonely. When he was gone, he wanted Lisette to be free. Unencumbered.

He pulled her arms from around his neck and made her stand. "Inside," he said. "Now. Please, Lizzy. Hurry."

Her eyebrows went up. I can't get out yet. I'm naked. Grab my suit."

"There's no one here but us. C'mon, Miss Priss. I'll guard your modesty. If anybody shows up unexpectedly, I'll throw myself on top of you so they can't see a thing."

She took his hand and followed him out of the pool, laughing. "You'd do that for me?"

He turned on the outdoor shower. "Anytime, day or night. All you have to do is ask."

They took turns rinsing off and then wrapped up in huge fluffy towels from a heated bin. Jonathan was nearing the edge of his self-control. It had been hours since he had made love to his brand-new wife, and he intended to make up for lost time.

Thirteen

Several hours after they left the pool, Lisette found herself standing with her sexy husband in a crowd of people at Shirley Heights, a restored military lookout and gun battery. This particular spot—just above their honeymoon villa—afforded incredible sunset views of English and Falmouth harbors. Every Sunday night the locals staged a huge barbecue, serenaded by a collection of home-grown musical talent.

Since it was the maid's day off, Jonathan had suggested this as a casual dinner plan. He held her close to his side as they made their way through the press of people. The tantalizing smells wafting from open grills and the pulsing rhythms of steel drums created a definite party atmosphere.

When they had eaten, they staked out a spot at the edge of the hilltop to witness the famed sunset. Lisette felt safe in Jonathan's embrace. She leaned against him, hoping to see the elusive green flash as the sun slid below the horizon. From this vantage point, it was fairly common, or so they had been told.

As they stood amid the throng of affable tourists, she felt the strangest combination of relaxation and arousal. Being here with Jonathan was the first truly carefree thing she had done for herself in years.

He smelled wonderful, a mix of warm male skin and elusive aftershave…something expensive, no doubt.

When someone bumped into them from behind, Lisette stumbled forward.

Jonathan steadied her. "You okay?"

She stretched her arms over her head, yawning. "I'm great," she said. "Oh, look. There it goes." The sun disappeared and, unmistakably, a brief burst of emerald lit the horizon.

"Maybe it's a good omen." Jonathan nuzzled her ear, standing behind her and sliding his arms around her waist.

"I never saw you as a superstitious kind of guy," she teased. It was true. The Jonathan Tarleton most people knew was logical and not given to flights of fancy. Yet here they were in a most unusual circumstance.

Darkness fell rapidly. They slowly made their way back to where Jonathan had parked the Jeep. "Ready for home, Ms. Tarleton?" he asked, helping her into the passenger seat. He paused to kiss her.

His lips were firm and warm, and tasted like cinnamon from the dessert they had shared.

When he pulled back at last and went around the Jeep to his own side, she put a hand to her chest, breathless.

They'd had sex twice so far today, and yet she trembled with wanting him.

At the house, she showered while Jonathan checked all the outer doors and turned on the overnight pool filter. When he returned, she was sitting in bed wearing another new purchase. The coffee-colored satin made her feel sexy and playful.

The flare of heat in Jonathan's eyes said he approved, as well. "I won't be long," he promised.

While she waited, she realized the two of them had a problem. They shouldn't use sex to manipulate each other. It wasn't productive, and it wasn't healthy. Jonathan had promised to think about the baby thing, but she didn't see any indication that he was changing his mind.

Maybe she would have to insist. Jonathan was going to have to make a few concessions. He had married her, and she wouldn't be kept in the dark about how he was feeling. If she was going to be at his side, he had to trust her. Completely.

Her serious musings evaporated when he strode nude across the bedroom and climbed into bed. It was still too soon for her to be blasé about his big, aroused, decidedly damp-from-the-shower body.

"Did you even *try* to dry off?" she asked.

He slipped a hand between her thighs, finding her warm center. "I was in a hurry." His other hand found a satin-covered breast and stroked it. "You look hot in this." His pupils were dilated. His ever-ready erection bobbed as if it hadn't been satisfied in months.

"Thank you."

He sprawled onto his back and lifted her across his body. "We started off like this earlier today and got sidetracked. Seeing you from this angle takes my breath away. You're gorgeous, Lizzy." He shimmied the satin up her thighs until it bunched around her waist.

She leaned forward and put her hands on his shoulders. "I like where this is going."

When he reached for the condom and handed it to her, his smile was challenging. "Will you do the honors?"

She hesitated. "If you want me to." Having him watch her so intently made the whole process nerve-racking. She handled the foil carefully. When it was time to roll the latex down his shaft, her hands trembled.

Jonathan, on the other hand, didn't move at all. He was rigid, braced as if to withstand mortal torture.

Her relative inexperience in this arena made the act unintentionally provocative. His chest heaved and he closed his eyes, groaning.

She flushed, more than a little turned-on by how very much he liked having her touch him. "I'm done," she said.

He opened one eyelid. "Oh, no, sweet thing. We're only just beginning."

Nothing he did was what she expected. Instead of lifting her onto his erection, he used his thumb to caress her intimately. She was embarrassingly wet. "I'm ready," she muttered, mortified by the fact that all her intimate bits were on full display.

His wicked smile calculated every degree of her insecurity. "You should see this from my side," he drawled. "Sheer perfection."

Her eyes scrunched shut, no longer able to watch his big tanned hands on her body. It was too much. Since she was trying very hard not to come yet, she started reciting multiplication tables in her head.

Jonathan seemed in no particular hurry to move past the overture. Now both of his thumbs separated her swollen labia. "I'm insane with wanting you, Lizzy. I'd swear you spiked my drink tonight if we hadn't been teetotalers."

His words were like sandpaper, scraping at her composure, revealing layers beneath. Truths she didn't want to admit. She went up on her knees and tried to move things along. When she wrapped her fingers around his shaft and guided him toward her entrance, every atom of air in the room dried up, leaving her breathless and starved for oxygen.

Gently she lowered herself until they were joined completely. The sensation of fullness from this angle was indescribable.

Jonathan's fingers gripped her bare butt so tightly she knew she would have bruises tomorrow. "Ride me, Lisette," he begged.

She was tentative at first, self-conscious. But Jonathan's response spurred her on. With her every careful slide downward, his sex found pleasure points inside her. "Jonathan…" She dropped her head back and closed her eyes.

He took the reins, a position she offered gladly. After that, all she had to do was feel and feel and feel. Each time they were together was different and new. Tonight he pushed her higher and higher, calculating which caresses would excite her without sending her over the top.

His own self-control seemed endless.

She was still wearing her nightgown. Jonathan was completely nude. The juxtaposition of her satin-clad flesh and his taut, muscled frame was provocative. Naughty.

When she managed a peek at him, his gaze burned into hers. "You're mine, Lizzy," he said.

A slight furrow creased her brow. The words sounded oddly possessive for a man who had nothing to offer her but his body…and that only temporarily. She glared at him through half-closed eyes. "Goes both ways, Jonathan. I want all of you. Nobody else. Just you."

Her words did something to him. He growled. There was no other way to describe the sound he made low in his throat. Bracing his feet against the mattress, he thrust wildly.

Lisette crashed over the edge of the precipice where he had kept her poised for hours, it seemed. The pleasure bordered on pain, sharp and deep.

Jonathan's climax racked his body, left him rigid and groaning. It lasted forever.

When she collapsed on top of him, her husband pulled the covers over them both. "Sleep," he muttered.

Lisette nodded and buried her face in the curve of his neck and shoulder. "Yes."

Monday dawned bright and glorious. Lisette didn't actually *see* the fabulous blue skies and sunshine until almost noon. Jonathan had awakened her twice during the night. Now she was sore and satiated and groggy.

When she realized that her husband was not in bed beside her, she frowned.

Before she could do anything more than run a hand through her wild sleep-tousled hair, Jonathan appeared in the doorway, looking disgustingly fresh and handsome. She felt like a wreck.

His gorgeous smile had her tugging the sheet upward instinctively. She needed sustenance before the next round. Were all honeymoons like this?

Then she focused on what he carried. A breakfast tray. Filled with an array of tantalizing goodies.

"May I ask you a favor?" she said politely.

His lips quirked in a grin. "Of course."

"Give me five minutes to freshen up. Then come back. And FYI, one pot of coffee might not be enough."

Her indefatigable lover chuckled, turned around and disappeared.

Fearing his level of cooperation, she darted from the bed and into the bathroom. Since her sexy nightgown was crumpled on the bedroom floor, she put on one of the thick terry robes, brushed her hair and washed her face.

By the time she returned to the bedroom, she felt marginally more human. Jonathan showed up as she sat down on the bed. She scooted toward the headboard and waited for him to place the breakfast tray across her lap.

She patted the mattress beside her. "You going to join me?"

"I'll have coffee," he said, pointing at the second cup. "I ate earlier. You were so tired I didn't want to wake you." His smug smile made her face heat.

"And whose fault was that?"

He mimicked her pose from the opposite side of the bed. "Mine. All mine."

Though he professed to have eaten, that didn't stop him from stealing tidbits from her tray. They shared the meal in companionable silence. The screened windows were open, letting in the breeze.

Lisette studied her husband when she thought he wasn't looking. He was young and healthy and strong.

At least that's what his outward appearance conveyed. She couldn't believe he was as sick as he said.

Maybe the culprit was stress. Here on vacation in a Caribbean playground he didn't appear to be in pain. His posture was relaxed, his color good. As soon as they returned to Charleston, she was going to try one more time to get him to another doctor for an evaluation.

People made mistakes all the time. Jonathan couldn't be dying. She wouldn't believe it.

When she declared herself stuffed, Jonathan removed the tray and sprawled beside her, head on his hand. In touching distance. Then he lifted one eyebrow. One sexy, inquisitive eyebrow.

"Oh, no," she said, laughing. "We need to pace ourselves. Besides, you promised me a tropical vacation. I've barely seen anything."

He put his hand on her ankle. "*I've* seen a lot," he smirked.

She stood before she could give in to temptation. After rounding the foot of the bed, she rummaged in her suitcase for a sundress. "What's on the agenda for today? And don't say sex," she warned, grinning in spite of herself.

The man had an enormous ego. It wouldn't be good for him to know how easily he could coax her into never leaving the house.

Jonathan pretended to be disappointed, but since he had showered and was wearing navy linen shorts and a collared shirt, she could tell he had an excursion in mind.

"I thought we'd go into St. John's," he said. "First of all, we need to buy wedding rings."

Her hands stilled in her suitcase. "That's not really necessary, is it?"

"We got married so quickly I had to improvise. But I want you look the part of the CEO's wife."

Any pleasure she had anticipated in the task, fizzled. "I see. That makes sense, I guess."

Inwardly she grimaced. The way he posed the shopping idea made it clear that his bargain with her was practical and not romantic. She knew that all too well. Still, disappointment soured her stomach.

Twenty minutes later they were headed down the hill and toward the capital. The city of twenty thousand plus was more cosmopolitan than Lisette had expected. Cruise ships docked regularly in the deep harbor. High-profile banks, upscale shops and malls all mingled with more traditional Antiguan enterprises. The spires of a cathedral dominated the skyline.

Jonathan parked and took her hand as they got out. "My friend who owns the villa told me where to find the best jeweler. I called ahead and told them we were coming."

Inside the small shop, well-lit cases were crammed with tray after tray of rings and necklaces and watches. Calypso music played from a room in the back. In a large cage dangling from the ceiling, a brightly colored parrot squawked a greeting. Unlike a glitzy establishment in the States, this enterprise was more pirate cove than Madison Avenue.

"Are you sure about this?" she whispered.

He nodded slowly. "I'm supposed to ask for Henry."

A large black man appeared from behind a curtain, beaming. "That would be me. And you, of course, are the Tarletons. Welcome to Antigua."

"Thank you," Jonathan said. "I'm Jonathan, and this is my wife, Lisette. We tied the knot in somewhat of a hurry, so we didn't have the appropriate rings. We're here to remedy that."

"Excellent. I have plenty of inventory, as you can see."

While the two men initiated a search, Lisette curled her fingers around the small signet ring on her left hand. She didn't really want to give it up. Jonathan had said vows to her and married her with this ring. It was special to her.

Reluctantly she slipped it off and tucked it into her small clutch purse.

When she joined the men at a case on the far side of the room, Henri had rolled out a red velvet cloth and was piling up choices, one after another. All the rings were in matching sets.

She shot Jonathan a startled glance. "*You're* going to wear a wedding band, too?"

"Of course." He seemed surprised. "Why wouldn't I?"

A dozen reasons came to mind right off. This wasn't a real marriage. He was only protecting his company and hiding his illness.

Fortunately, his question was rhetorical and didn't require an answer.

Henry spoke up, his British accent most appealing. "Do you see anything you like, little ma'am?"

"Those are nice," she said, pointing to a plain set, hoping they would be less expensive. It seemed both reckless and immoral to spend a fortune on a prop.

Jonathan nodded. "I like them, as well."

The shiny silver-colored bands were edged with the tiniest of beading design around the rims.

The jeweler handed both rings to Jonathan. "Platinum. Designer pieces. Excellent choice."

Before Lisette could protest the expense, Jonathan took her hand in his and slipped the smaller of the two rings on her left hand without ceremony. It fit perfectly.

He smiled at her. "What do you think?"

"It's lovely."

Instead of offering her the male ring—so she could return the favor—he put the second band on his own finger and nodded. "These will do nicely. Now we need to look at engagement rings."

Lisette pulled on his arm. "May I speak to you in private?"

Jonathan frowned. "Right now?"

"Yes, right now."

While Henry straightened the case, Lisette dragged Jonathan over toward the front door of the shop. She lowered her voice. "I don't want an engagement ring. Under the circumstances, it's completely unnecessary."

Jonathan's eyes turned glacial. He wasn't accustomed to anyone countermanding his wishes. "Under *what* circumstances?"

"Don't be deliberately dense. This is a marriage of expedience, of convenience. It's pointless to spend thousands of dollars on a meaningless romantic gesture."

He was stone cold now. *This* was the man she knew the best. The unflappable CEO. The hard-edged businessman.

"And what about the honeymoon?"

She cocked her head, confused. What about it?"

"Wouldn't you say the honeymoon has been real?"

His icy gaze dropped from her face to her breasts. "Surely that deserves recognition."

Her temper flared. "When a man has sex with a woman and then pays her off in pricey baubles, there's a word for that."

His chin jutted. "You're my wife, not some random woman. I fail to see why my buying you a diamond makes me the bad guy."

"I'd rather have a baby than a diamond ring."

Here they were again. Back at square one. Arguing. Apparently, the only time they were both in perfect accord was when they were in bed.

Her throat was tight with sad, angry tears. And the truth was even worse. She wasn't angry with Jonathan for being who he was; she was angry with herself for falling into the trap of believing any of this was real.

She lowered her head, not wanting him to see her anguish. "Fine," she muttered. "Pick one out. I'll wear it."

The standoff lasted for painful seconds. Then, with a low curse, Jonathan whirled around and went back to confer with the jeweler again.

Because Lisette refused to be part of the process, she lingered where she was, pretending to peruse the collection of watches. If Henry was puzzled by her indifference, he didn't let on. Fifteen minutes later, he and Jonathan completed their transaction.

Outside, the sun was blinding. Lisette donned her sunglasses. "Can we do lunch next?" she asked. "I'm getting hungry."

"Not yet." Without warning, Jonathan knelt in the street and took her hand. "Lisette Stanhope, will you do me the honor of being engaged to me?"

Fourteen

Jonathan knew he was in trouble. He had hurt his bride—not intentionally, but nevertheless true. Now he willingly made a fool of himself in hopes of bringing a smile back to her face.

She wanted a baby, and Lord knows, he'd enjoy making one with her. Something stopped him though. A certainty that it wasn't fair to tie her down when he wouldn't be around to share the parenting.

Lisette pulled on his arm. "Get up, for goodness' sake. People are staring at us."

He allowed her to pull him to his feet, but still he held the ring. "I asked you a question, Lizzy. My execution was faulty all along the way, but no less sincere. Say you'll marry me."

She gaped at him, and then her mouth snapped shut. "We're *already* married. This is ridiculous."

"When is your birthday?"

"It was three weeks ago, remember? I took the day off and went to Savannah with a friend."

"Ah, yes." Again he took her hand. "Then consider this a belated birthday present. It wouldn't have been an appropriate gift from your boss, but now it's perfectly acceptable." Before she could protest, he reached out and slid the ring onto the third finger of her left hand. "Happy two-day anniversary, Ms. Tarleton. Here's to many more."

For the first time, Lisette looked at the ring. Her eyes widened.

Jonathan had selected a stunning stone, emerald cut. Three carats. Virtually perfect in color and clarity. The delicate setting did nothing to detract from the diamond's beauty. As Lisette held up her arm, the sun caught facets of the once-upon-a-time carbon and cast rainbows in every direction.

"Do you like it?" he asked. "We don't have to keep it. We can get something else. But I want you to have something as beautiful as you are."

Lisette grabbed him around his neck, nearly strangling him. "How is it that I'm ready to murder you one minute and kiss you the next?"

Her aggrieved question made him laugh. He folded her close against his chest. "It's not an easy thing we're doing," he said, stroking her hair, the strands hot from the sun. "I plunged us into this arrangement without much thought. We'll muddle through, I swear."

She pulled back and kissed him sweetly, healing the rift between them. "I'm sorry I was so grumpy," she said. "Thank you for my engagement ring."

Every time he took her in his arms, he wanted her.

In a bed. Standing up against a brick wall in a nearby alley. He shook his head, dislodging the fantasy. "Thank *you*," he said. "For wearing it."

Their détente lasted all through lunch. They found a place by the water and dined on fat prawns, sourdough bread and coleslaw. At his insistence, Lisette enjoyed a glass of wine with her meal.

Her eyes sparkled with happiness.

The truth struck him without warning. Like a tsunami barreling in from the sea, flattening every preconception in its wake.

He was in love with his bride. In lust, yes. But even more than that.

His heart hammered in his chest. The prawns rolled restlessly in his stomach. This wasn't part of the equation, part of the agreement. Suddenly, the idea of making Lisette pregnant seemed the most logical thing in the world.

He had chosen her to be his temporary bride because she was an impartial bystander. It was a lie he had told himself instead of admitting the truth. He wanted her and needed her.

Since he couldn't promise her forever, maybe giving her a baby was the best way to show her how much he cared.

She reached across the table and touched his hand. "You okay?"

Even the innocent caress of her fingers made him hollow with need. He nodded jerkily. "Sorry. My mind wandered."

Lisette made a face. "Not to business, I hope. We'll have to deal with all of that soon enough."

He made himself return her smile though it felt false.

"Indeed. Today, we play. Did I mention that my buddy has a cabin cruiser…a small yacht? I thought we'd take her out for a spin."

"I'd love that," she said, her enthusiasm infectious. "Now I know why you insisted we bring our beach bags."

He nodded. "I wanted to surprise you, but I didn't think you'd go for nude sunbathing, even in the middle of the ocean."

"Not enough sunscreen in the world for that," she said, chuckling.

They left the Jeep parked in a shady spot on a quiet side street and made their way to the marina on foot. The formalities were brief though thorough. Afterward they changed clothes in the public cabana-like restroom. Soon they were motoring their way out of the harbor at a snail's pace, heading toward open water.

Lisette shoved her hair up under a floppy cloth hat.

"Better tie it," he said. "Or the wind will snatch it away."

When he cleared the final no-wake sign, he opened the throttle. Lisette had chosen to sit at the bow of the boat with her face to the horizon. When the vessel picked up velocity, practically dancing over the water as if the craft were airborne, the wind snatched her laughter and carried it back to him where he stood at the wheel.

He understood her response. It wasn't humor. It was the sheer exhilaration of speed.

For half an hour he ranged around the coastline. This vantage point gave them a new perspective. Antigua was a blue-and-green jewel dotted with white-sand beaches, 365 in all, or so the tourist bureau would have you believe.

At last he cut the engine and let the craft bob on the open water.

Lisette turned around. "Are you dropping anchor?"

"No. Too deep. But we're fine where we are. You want something to drink? Maybe you should get out of the sun for a little while. Your cute nose is turning pink."

She made her way back toward the rear of the boat, staggering once when a choppy wave slapped the hull. "Is *get out of the sun* code for fooling around? I've never had sex on a boat."

"Have a seat." He handed her a water bottle, grinning. "I might be persuaded. Though I warn you, the bunks below are narrow."

Lisette drained the bottle and rested her head against the back of the cushioned banquette. "I could live like this," she said, eyes closed, expression dreamy.

He studied her intently, noting the way her white lacy cover-up billowed in the breeze, giving him tantalizing peeks of bare skin. "I never can decide which I like best—the flat-out exhilaration of speed or the challenge of battling the wind in a sailboat."

She peeked over her shoulder at the harbor in the distance. "Sailboats are beautiful. But I'd probably be one of those people who misjudges the boom and gets bumped into the water."

She stood and padded toward him in her bare feet, wrapping both arms around his waist. He folded her close. "I'd never let that happen to you, Lizzy." He bent his head and kissed her lazily, enjoying the slow buzz of arousal, the perfect bliss of a summer afternoon.

There wasn't a cloud on the horizon. The only storms up ahead were the ones he faced personally. Holding her like this made him want to fight for his future. But what was the point? Trying to stave off the inevitable would only drag both of them through a painful, uncertain time.

It was better to stay with the course he had chosen. Live each day to the fullest for as long as he had. He would love her and care for her the only way he knew how. And if a baby came from that love, perhaps the child would be a far more lasting legacy than a shipping business.

When Lisette went downstairs to visit the head, Jonathan stared out to sea. For a brief moment, he flashed on a snippet of memory from his younger days. He and Hartley had been barely fifteen, thinking they ruled the world. A friend had offered them his sailboat for the afternoon.

Both boys were experienced boaters, but a storm had blown up out of nowhere, turning the ocean into a raging beast. They had barely made it back into dock. The near miss had sobered them.

Without Hartley by his side, Jonathan might have died.

And now he was going to die without his twin anyway. The sharp pain in his chest was bittersweet. Holding onto anger was exhausting and pointless. He'd closed the book on Hartley months ago. He no longer had a brother.

When Lisette reappeared, he shook off his melancholy. "You ready to move on?"

She pretend-pouted, looking adorably sexy and playful. "I checked out those bunks. They're not so bad."

His body tightened. "I'm listening."

He'd been keeping the boat in relatively the same orientation, idling the motor occasionally and adjusting their position relative to the island. But it wouldn't hurt to drift briefly.

Lisette took off her cover-up and swimsuit top. "A quickie to hold us over until we get back to the house? I'm pretty sure this is a bucket list item."

Her challenging smile was adorable. Did she really think he had any objections? Hell, no. The sight of her soft, full breasts—completely bare—dried his mouth.

He shut off the engine and locked the wheel. "Five minutes," he said. He scanned the horizon. "We're all alone at the moment. No danger in sight." Except his wife's delectable body. "Down the steps, woman. I'm right behind you."

Lizzy started laughing when he tried to undress and slammed his elbow into a cabinet door. Pain shot up his arm, but he was undeterred.

She shimmied out of her swimsuit bottom and scooted onto the nearest berth. The simple navy cotton comforter was covered with a white nautical print. The vision in front of him looked like some kind of erotic pinup girl from a sailor's calendar.

"Hurry up," she said huskily. "You said five minutes."

Fast wasn't going to be a problem. He was on a hair trigger. Suddenly he ground his jaw and kicked the side of the bunk, barely even flinching when his toes protested.

Lisette's eyes widened. "What's wrong?"

"No condoms, damn it."

"Oh." She pulled the covers over her naked body,

clearly trying to mask her disappointment with a wobbly smile. "Then we'll wait. No worries."

He fought a battle with himself. He couldn't tell her how he felt. Not with his diagnosis. His love would be nothing more than a burden. There was one thing he could do, and that was give her the baby she wanted. It hurt like hell to think he wouldn't know his own child. But it hurt even more to know he wouldn't be able to love Lizzy the way she deserved.

"Jonathan?" She lifted up on her elbows, a familiar pose. It made her look like temptation incarnate, though this time she kept the covers clutched to her chest.

"Do you still want to get pregnant?" he asked bluntly.

The color drained from her face and then rushed back in a flush of red that covered her cheeks and throat and everything else he could see. "Is that a serious question?"

His arms hung at his sides, hands fisted. He was so hard he ached all the way from his balls to his teeth. "Completely."

Her smile was radiant, nearly knocking him on his ass with its voltage. "Yes, Jonathan. I do."

"Okay, then. Let's do this." His world shifted into a weird pinpoint focus. Time slowed. He levered himself onto the narrow berth alongside her, pausing to assess the situation. When he slipped a finger into her sex, she was ready for him. More than ready.

His options were limited. This boat wasn't built for Kama Sutra positions. Jonathan moved on top of his lover and entered her steadily. "Good God," he whispered, fully reverent.

She smoothed the hair from his damp forehead with a gentle caress. "What, Jonathan? Tell me."

He kissed her temple, her nose, her soft, perfect lips. "I've never been with a woman like this. Skin to skin."

Her gaze reflected the wonderment he felt. "I like it," she confessed almost bashfully. "But you know it will take more than once."

"We'll just have to work at it," he groaned. "I'm game if you are."

She stroked his back, her fingernails digging into his flesh when he surged hard inside her. The little hiccupped moan she made inflamed him. In this most elemental joining, he felt his control slip far too soon. *Hell*. The additional stimulation without a manmade barrier dragged him deep into a place of drugged pleasure so dizzying he might never find his way back to the surface.

His climax hit hard and went on forever, until he was drained. He slumped on top of his bride. Vaguely he remembered hearing her come.

They were both covered in sweat. In the distance, the mournful cry of a seagull drew him back to consciousness.

Grief hit him hard. He adored his bride and he didn't want to give her up. Ever. How could he say goodbye to her? How could he imagine another man stepping in one day and living the life that was supposed to be Jonathan's.

How could he lose everything he cared about?

He shifted to one side and cupped her cheek with his hand. "Did I crush you?"

Her green eyes stared up at him, dazed. "Wow."

"Yeah. Wow." That about summed it up.

He toyed with her navel. "I should probably make sure everything is okay on deck."

She nodded. "You do that. I'll just stay here and reminisce."

"Brat." He reached for his shirt and swim shorts and reluctantly abandoned her. Taking the ladder two rungs at a time, he vaulted upward.

Nothing had changed. The sea still moved mysteriously beneath the hull. The sun continued to beam down with heat and passion.

But, for Jonathan, everything had been upended. He was going to fight. He wasn't going to take no for an answer when it came to pursuing other treatment options. And he was going pray like hell that his make-believe wife might fall in love with him for real.

He wanted to *tell* Lizzy, to thank her for rescuing him from despair. To prove to her that he wanted to make their marriage real. A forever kind of deal. But something held him back. In business, he never rolled out a new initiative unless he had studied every angle.

That's how he would handle this new decision. No point in getting Lisette's hopes up. It would only disappoint both of them if there really was no hope for his recovery.

He started the engine and studied the radar. Good depth. No problems.

When Lisette joined him, her smile was hard to read. It wasn't smug, and it wasn't jubilant.

If anything, she seemed cautiously pleased. Come to think of it, that was a pretty damn good description of how *he* felt at the moment.

She stood beside him and repaired her ponytail with practiced feminine movements. "Do we have plenty of gas?"

He glanced at the gauge. "Yes. Why?"

She sighed and leaned her head on his shoulder, wrapping her arm through his. "I want to go fast again."

His wife had a need for speed. He understood that desire perfectly. "All you had to do was ask." As she released him and headed for the bow again, he raised his voice to be heard over the revving motor. "Promise me you'll hold on to the rail. I don't want to lose you."

She half turned, gazing at him over her shoulder, her expression mischievous. "You're never going to lose me, Jonathan Tarleton. I'm yours until the last sunset. Now let's get going. See if you can make me scream."

The taunting double entendre made him laugh. "Challenge accepted."

When he was sure she was settled with one hand clenched around the railing, he let the beast loose. He would never be careless with his passenger. He knew exactly how far he could push the nimble pleasure craft.

The needles on all the dials quivered and moved to the right. His eyes stung even behind sunglasses. The wind in his face was surprisingly cold.

He shouted at her. "More?"

She nodded, lifting one hand and pointing at the sky.

If he had his way, he would have taken Lizzy all the way beyond the horizon in search of a happy ending. Instead, he did the next best thing. He let her feel what it was like to fly.

Seconds passed. Minutes. He was vigilant. Eagle-eyed. One wrong move could mean a collision with another craft. But he kept them just inside the edge of reason. It was exhilarating and cathartic and utterly perfect.

He noted the rapidly dwindling fuel supply and realized that it was time to go back. One more minute. One more dose of immortality.

Disaster struck without warning. A stabbing pain crushed the back of his right eye. His vision blurred. Anguished incredulity shook him. *Please, God, no. Not now.*

Instinctively he backed off on the throttle. Too quickly, in fact. He stumbled and had to grab the counter for purchase. Lisette ended up in the floor of the boat, laughing. "You could have warned me," she called out.

He gripped the wheel, barely able to see. "Lizzy. I need you to come back here."

She waved him off. "I'm fine," she said. "Don't worry. It wasn't that much of a bump. I'm not hurt."

Sweat poured down his back. The pain made him want to throw up. But that would scare her.

Think, man, think.

Slowly, stifling a groan, he reached for a water bottle and uncapped it. He tried a sip, but his stomach rebelled. Instead, he poured it around his neck. His heart rate was in the stratosphere. Shock, no doubt.

They were too far from shore. Too damned far.

He raised his voice a second time. "Lizzy. I need you to come back here. Now. Please."

Fifteen

Lisette's head snapped around. Her stomach clenched in alarm. The note in Jonathan's voice was so utterly unlike him she knew something was badly wrong. After leaping to her feet, she ran back to where he stood.

"What is it?" she cried, panicked by his pallor. "What is it?" But she knew. Dear God in heaven, she knew.

He was gritting his teeth, gray and shaking. "Something happened to my right eye."

"You're in pain?"

His brief hesitation was telling. "Yes. I can't see much on that side."

She removed his sunglasses and put them in the cup holder on the dash. "Take my hand," she said softly, speaking to him as she would a frightened child. "Sit down, Jonathan."

He slumped onto the bench seat, barely upright.

"You'll have to get us back in. I'll help you with the boat."

"I don't care about the damn boat," she yelled, forgetting her bedside manner. Tears stung her eyes. "Tell me you have medicine with you, damn it. Tell me you do."

He nodded jerkily. "Foil packet. In my wallet. I can't take both. They knock me out. The doctor gave them to me for emergencies."

Her hands were shaking as she riffled through the pockets of his windbreaker and found his billfold. Jonathan was in pain. She couldn't bear it.

At last she found the tablets and punched one through the foil. When she handed it over and offered him water, he managed to swallow the medicine with a grimace.

"You feel sick, don't you?" she said.

"A little." The lie was not even close to being believable.

What would they do if he couldn't keep the pills down? "Don't move for a few minutes."

"Okay." He slid until he was on his back with one arm flung across his eyes. The canopy protected them from the sun.

Suddenly she realized that the motor was still puttering at low speed. Instead of asking Jonathan, she studied the dashboard, located the appropriate controls and shut off the engine.

Now they bobbed in the water. Alone in a great expanse of blue.

"Do I need to call for help?" she asked quietly.

The muscles in his throat rippled visibly. "No."

Even ill and hurting, he was utterly masculine. He had one tanned leg extended on the seat. The other foot braced on the floor of the boat.

She knelt beside him and rested her cheek against his arm. "Take your time. We're not in a rush."

When he stroked her hair, she could tell his hand was shaking.

Minutes passed. Five. Ten. Thirty. Under other circumstances, this lazy summer float would have been relaxing. As it was, Lisette's stomach cramped in painful knots. She was so damned scared. Not for herself, but for Jonathan.

At last he struggled to sit up. A bit of color had returned to his face, and he no longer looked as if he were about to pass out.

When he had both feet on the floor, she put her hands on his knees. "Look at me, Jonathan. And don't give me some pretty lie. How bad is your head?"

He covered her hands with his. "Bearable."

"You swear?"

His smile didn't quite reach his eyes. "I swear."

She nodded. "Okay then. Tell me what to do."

Slowly he straightened, swaying only slightly, though that could have been the motion of the boat. "I'll be right here beside you. We'll take it easy. This dial needs to stay between these two lines. The only tricky part will be entering the harbor. It's going to be busy."

"I'm fine," she said. "I've always wanted to learn how to drive a yacht."

He winced, this time theatrically. "You don't *drive* a yacht."

She waved a hand. "Whatever. Now lie back down and rest.

Though they were only a few miles offshore, at the speed where Lisette felt comfortable, it was going to take at least half an hour or more. Gradually the island began to come into focus. She wasn't sure which was scarier—being in control of a huge watercraft in the middle of the ocean, or coming closer to land, and having to navigate an obstacle course of Jet Skis and sailboats and a dozen other yachts and speedboats of every shape and size.

Jonathan stayed upright the entire way, not standing but seated inches away from her, his mere presence giving her the confidence she needed.

Once they reached the mouth of the harbor, she cut their speed even more and clutched the steering wheel. "Here goes nothing," she muttered.

"You're doing great."

A few vessels honked at her for going *too* slow, but for the most part, her progress was unimpeded. When they approached the area of the marina where the yacht had been berthed, her nerves increased. "I hope your friend has insurance. This is worse than parallel parking."

"I'll help you," Jonathan said. "It will be fine." He rose to his feet and muttered something.

She shot him a look, alarmed. "What's wrong?"

The jut of his jawline was grim. "My depth perception is shot. We'll have to get close and drift in. The guys at the dock will tie us off."

The next fifteen minutes were a blur. Somehow, Lisette managed to get the boat close enough to the pier for Jonathan to throw a rope. His first try landed in the water. A second attempt worked.

When Jonathan reached over and cut the engine, Lisette exhaled a noisy sigh. "Never again," she said. Instead of feeling relief, now she was free to worry about her husband.

He kissed her sweaty cheek. "You were great." When he bent down and started gathering their personal items, she gritted her teeth. Stubborn man.

"Let me do that," she said, trying to elbow him out of the way.

"Lisette." The steel in his voice told her the CEO was back. "I'm fine." The unspoken message was *Back off.*

But he was definitely *not* fine. She knew that the worst part of today's ordeal for him had been feeling out of control. Now he was trying to take over again, though she was damned if she would let him collapse in the street.

Because he was ignoring her attempts to make him sit down, she got in his face and glared. "Here's the schedule, big guy. We're going to slowly stroll to our car. I'll drive us back to the villa. Then we'll have a peaceful, quiet dinner and make a game plan."

"Why do we need a plan? If you're insisting I rest, let's spend all day by the pool tomorrow. Problem solved."

She gaped at him, unable to tell if he was serious or merely trying to aggravate her. "The honeymoon is over, Jonathan. We're flying home to Charleston as soon as I can get that swanky jet back down here. I may need your help with the details," she conceded.

Jonathan picked up the large straw tote and motioned her ahead of him. "You go first. And take somebody's hand when you climb out. The boat can move unexpectedly."

A dozen strong feelings duked it out in her chest, not the least of which was the furious impulse to push her aggravating husband overboard and let him take his chances.

Because she didn't want to make a scene—and because several gorgeous dock hands were waiting to secure the boat and return it to its assigned slip—Lisette picked up the small cooler and climbed out.

She wasn't able to breathe until Jonathan was on dry land, as well. Of *course*, he hadn't asked for help disembarking.

The afternoon heat was blistering. Earlier she'd had the impression they parked close to the water. Now, the distance seemed to have multiplied.

Jonathan walked beside her, not saying a word. She wanted to ask how he was feeling, but she didn't want to get her head snapped off.

When they reached the car at last, she put a small towel down on the driver's seat to keep from burning her legs on the hot leather. Jonathan's movements were *careful* as he eased into the passenger seat. She had the impression he was trying to limit his range of motion to keep from jostling his head.

At the villa, she parked haphazardly and faced her silent passenger. "Go straight to the bedroom. Please, Jonathan. I'll check with the maid about our dinner. Then I'll come join you, and we can talk."

He nodded. His pallor had increased again, despite the humid temperature. When she found him half an hour later, he was sprawled on top of the mattress, facedown, as if the strength of his will had carried him that far but no farther.

She whispered his name. When there was no answer, she leaned down to make sure he was breathing. The fear she had kept at bay earlier came rushing back. The doctor had said six months. Jonathan had been feeling pretty good lately. Surely this was a momentary setback.

Or maybe it was the beginning of the end.

She gathered fresh clothes, went into the bathroom and locked the door. Then she stood in a hot shower and cried. Jonathan had married her because he needed someone calm and capable in his corner. Somehow she had to find it in herself to ignore her own grief and be the woman he needed.

When she finally returned to the bedroom, she was blissfully clean but puffy eyed, Hopefully, Jonathan wouldn't notice.

She found him on his back this time, staring at the ceiling.

Though it seemed impossible under the circumstances, she wanted him still. She needed the physical connection to reassure herself she wasn't losing him yet. Today had been both terrifying and illuminating. Jonathan had been an integral part of her life for many years. Now he was her husband. Whatever happened to him was going to impact every part of her existence.

She scooted across the bed, huddled into her robe, and curled up beside him, resting her head on the edge of his pillow. Immediately he shifted and put his arm around her, still silent.

When she found the courage to speak, there was no point in playing games. "You know we have to go home…right?"

"I know." The flat intonation in those two words could have masked anger or despair or both.

"We should call your sister and brother-in-law and ask them to come over for dinner tomorrow night. Mazie's going to realize something is up when we return home early. The explanations will be better face-to-face."

"That's why I married you," he said lightly. "The voice of wisdom."

"You don't sound glad. That was a pretty snarky comment."

He rolled to his feet. "How long till dinner?"

"Half an hour."

"I'll shower and meet you on the terrace."

As a dismissal, it was unmistakable. She swallowed her hurt. "I'll use the guest room to finish getting ready."

"Suit yourself." It was as if he couldn't bear to look at her. "I'll be out shortly."

Jonathan was being an asshole. He recognized the behavior, but he couldn't seem to do anything about it.

He wanted to hide from the world, from Lisette in particular.

His *episode* today had completely knocked the wind out of him. He'd thought he had time. He'd thought things would only get bad at the end. Apparently he'd been in denial all along.

How could he know what was right and what was wrong? Lisette wanted a baby. Maybe they had created a new life today. But if not, surely it was for the best. Time was running out for him. Bit by bit he was losing everything. Knowing that his future with Lisette was slipping between his fingers stabbed him with painful regret.

Though the last thing he felt like doing was eating some fancy romantic meal, he couldn't bring himself to abandon his bride in the midst of their honeymoon. He joined her as promised. It didn't escape his notice that Lisette downed three glasses of wine during dinner.

He wasn't the only one who had suffered today. Lisette must have been scared out of her mind, but the woman was a damned trouper. She'd kept her cool, and she had done what had to be done.

Tonight she looked like a weary angel. Her halter-necked sundress was pale peach, a soft color that made her sun-kissed skin glow. She had put her hair up, exposing the vulnerable nape of her neck.

As crappy as the day had been, Jonathan knew how he wanted it to end. With Lizzy beneath him, welcoming him home. He loved her. Truth be told, he was only now realizing how much. Faced with the prospect of losing her, his feelings were a riotous flood of thoughts and yearnings he dared not reveal.

But would she desire him the same way tonight?

A man liked to be a man. Today hadn't shown him at his best. Would she think less of him? The random thought didn't even make sense. His emotions were all over the place.

He ate enough to be sociable and then nursed a glass of water while picking at his dessert. The mango sorbet and shortbread cookie were delicious, though he'd lost his appetite along with his faith in the future.

The maid came been back and forth, serving and removing dishes. Her interruptions kept the awkward lack of conversation between bride and groom at bay. But now dinner was over and the silence lengthened.

Jonathan felt the weight of everything piling up on him. His wife. His company. His sister and J.B. and the old man. How was it all going to play out? Would Hartley try to swoop in and take over? His brother's motives were still a painful mystery.

Jonathan never should have asked for Lisette's help.

She didn't deserve this. She needed a man who was whole. One who could give her multiple children and a home and a happily-ever-after.

His mood slipped lower. All the positive thinking in the world wasn't going to change a damn thing.

He stood abruptly and tossed his napkin on the table. "I'm going for a walk," he said gruffly. "Don't wait up for me."

"I could go with you."

His shoulders tensed as he stopped with his back to her. Tense seconds passed. "No. I'd rather be alone right now."

Lisette made some excuse to the maid and fled inside. To have her husband make it so embarrassingly clear he didn't want her company was a pain that left her breathless. She was no psychologist, but she recognized why Jonathan was pushing her away.

Perhaps it was the only choice he could make to deal with the changes happening in his life. The terrifying moment out on the water today would have frightened anyone. For a man who kept an iron grip on his destiny, the incident must surely have made the earth shift beneath his feet.

She gathered everything she needed and holed up in the guest suite across the hall from the master bedroom. The hollow feeling in her chest wouldn't go away. After changing into the soft feminine nightwear she had bought for her honeymoon, she sat on the bed, scooted up against the headboard and tried to read the novel she had brought with her.

The book was a bestseller by one of her favorite

comedic writers. After she read the same page three times, she gave up.

Was she going to be reduced to playing online solitaire during her honeymoon?

She picked up her cell phone and nearly dropped it when it rang insistently. No contact was linked to the number, but it was a Charleston-area prefix, so she answered.

"Hello?"

After the briefest of pauses, a male voice on the other end spoke. "Lisette, this is Hartley Tarleton, Jonathan's brother."

Her gasp was loud enough for him to hear. "Why are you calling me? How did you get this number?" She had been with Tarleton Shipping long before Hartley disappeared, so she knew him, of course. But they weren't on casual phone-call terms.

"Mazie gave it to me. Listen, Lisette. I need to know about Jonathan. He's in trouble isn't he? Tell me what's going on. Mazie says he's sick."

"Why would you think he's in trouble?" Her mind raced feverishly, looking for sinister motives in the conversation.

Hartley's muttered curse was audible, even with a crackly cell connection. "He's my twin. We've always had that gut ESP thing. Quit stalling. I need to know."

"You shouldn't be calling me," she said, trying to sound firm when her insides were shaking. "Ask your sister."

"I did, damn it. Mazie gave me the bare bones, but she said you're the one who knows everything that's going on with my brother…all the details."

"Well, she's wrong. Your brother isn't big on opening up to people. Or have you forgotten that?"

"I haven't forgotten anything."

"I'm hanging up now," she whispered. "Jonathan would be furious if he knew I was talking to you. Whatever you did hurt him very badly."

There was a brief pause where she could hear Hartley breathing. Then he spoke softly. "Jonathan wasn't the only one who got hurt, Lisette. Think about that, why don't you. And if you have any heart at all, swear you'll let me know when the situation gets bad. I have to be there with him. Please."

"I can't promise that."

"I love him."

The three words were filled with such aching anguish that tears stung her eyes. "I do, too," Lisette said.

"Keep my number."

She knew she shouldn't. She knew it was wrong. But she felt a strong, empathetic connection to Jonathan's banished sibling. "I will. But that's all I can promise, Hartley. I'm sorry." She tapped the red button and ended the call before she could change her mind.

Sixteen

The adrenaline and stress of the day left their mark on Lisette. After the odd phone call with Hartley, she fell asleep almost instantly, though she tossed restlessly and turned the sheets into a tangled mess.

Sometime after one in the morning, a noise jerked her awake.

Jonathan's whisper soothed her fears. "It's me, Lizzy." He scooped her into his arms and carried her to their bedroom. "I'm sorry I was an ass. I can't sleep without you."

She curled against him, relief flooding her body. "Don't shut me out." She wanted to tell him she loved him, but she stopped short.

"I'll try," he said.

His arms were strong, cradling her to his naked chest. He smelled like soap and warm male skin and everything she held dear.

"Are you okay?" she asked. He'd told her not to do that…not to hover and ask questions about his health. But her need to know was stronger than her worry about his displeasure.

After a moment's pause, he kissed her forehead and deposited her gently on their bed. At some point he had carefully folded back the sheets before coming to the other room. Now he joined her and stretched out with a sigh. "I'm fine."

She raised up on one elbow, stroking the hair from his forehead, only then realizing that he was *completely* nude. "Truly?"

"Truly."

His expression was hard to read. A night-light burned in the adjoining bathroom, but the bedroom itself was shadowed and dim. "Did you make arrangements for the jet?" she asked. Surely that was a safe topic.

He nodded. "We'll need to be at the airport by ten thirty tomorrow morning for preflight security and screening."

Suddenly she knew what she had to do, what she *wanted* to do. "Then we have tonight," she whispered. If their honeymoon was to be cut short, she wanted him to remember these last few hours…to remember her as his bride. When they returned to Charleston, she couldn't bear it if he pushed her aside in his quest to be stoic. She needed him to understand they were a team.

She braced herself on one hand and bent her head to taste a flat, copper-colored nipple. With her free hand, she stroked the hard planes of his chest. His abdomen was roped with impressive muscles. "I love your body," she murmured, feeling the texture that was so uniquely male. Warm silk over taut sinew.

Jonathan shuddered when she touched him intimately. He tried to move on top of her, but she pushed him back. "Let me do this first, Jonathan. I want to... please."

He closed his eyes, his entire body rigid. She circled the head of his sex with her tongue, loving the sounds he made when she took more of him in her mouth. Here, in their bedroom, she breached his careful barriers. Here, in the dark of night, he let her see his wants. His needs.

Maybe his thoughts were still hidden from her. Maybe they always would be. But at least in this one place, they knew each other fully.

The hour was late. Though Lisette wanted to make the pleasure last for hours, Jonathan was too hungry, too reluctant to play the submissive forever. When he groaned and cursed and fisted his hands in the sheets, his control snapped so quickly it caught her off guard.

"No more," he rasped. He stripped her flimsy gown away. "On your back, woman. Let me see you."

She smiled up at him. "Nothing has changed. All the parts are still the same."

He shook his head slowly. "That's where you're wrong. Each time I take you, I swear you dazzle me more. Your body is soft and curved and perfect, but that's not even the best of it. You're smart and funny and strong, and all those things pale in comparison to your huge heart."

Her mouth dropped open. She had never heard him speak so poetically. In fact, she didn't know he had it in him. Her eyes misted. "What a lovely thing to say."

His smile was lopsided. "It's all true." He cupped her breast in his hand. "Now, at the risk of undoing all my fine words, I'm going to take you hard and fast, because I've wanted you for hours, Lizzy, and I'm afraid I might die if I don't get inside you soon."

It was just an expression. A funny way of expressing his arousal. But her throat tightened. "I want you just as badly, Jonathan Tarleton." She pulled his head down for a kiss. "I'm all yours."

Relief made him light-headed. Lizzy was being far more generous that he might have been were their situations reversed. She hadn't taken him to task for his grouchy behavior earlier. Her empathy made him want to be a better man.

Though his erection ached and throbbed, he made himself wait. He would show her how much she meant to him even if he couldn't say the words. After tucking an extra pillow beneath her head, he gave himself free rein to pleasure her until neither of them could bear any more.

He had rapidly grown addicted to the feel of her skin beneath his fingertips. The fragrance of her shampoo. The way her spine arched off the bed when he found a spot on the inside of her thigh that made her tremble.

He tasted every inch of her skin, knew every soft, damp secret.

Deliberately he drove her higher and higher, holding her ruthlessly on the knife edge of release, denying them both what they wanted.

When she moaned his name and wrapped her arms around his neck, he knew the time had come. He settled between her thighs and fit the head of his sex at her entrance. "Watch," he said. "Watch me take you."

Her pupils were dilated, almost covering her irises.

He had kissed her so long and so hard her lips were pink and swollen. When she looked down at the spot where their bodies joined, she nodded slowly, her expression arrested. "Yes, Jonathan. Yes."

He entered her slowly, perhaps more slowly than he ever had before. Each tiny increment was exquisite torture. Her body gripped his, knew his. The connection was more than physical. It was painfully real and encompassing, and if he hadn't been drowning in sheer physical bliss, he might have run screaming from the knowledge that he hadn't managed to hold anything back from her.

He was losing himself completely.

When he was lodged inside her all the way, he hesitated. Most of his weight rested on his arms so as not to crush her. "Lizzy?"

"Yes?" Her expression was unguarded. Open. Revealing. Was that love he saw there? He wanted it to be so. He wanted to believe that Lizzy was with him because she needed him, not the other way around. He had kept so much of himself closed off for so long, it was habit now. He craved her love. Yearned for it.

Fear held him back. Fear of being weak. Fear that he would fail her by leaving her alone. "Never mind," he muttered. "It will keep."

He withdrew and thrust deep, sending both of them into delirium. It might have been hours or minutes that he moved wildly inside her, relishing the way her inner muscles clutched at him as if trying to link them forever. The sensation was exquisite and painful, and his body ached and shuddered and finally exploded.

Lizzy came, too. He heard her cry, felt the way her

legs wrapped around his waist and her body lifted into him, trying to ride every last trembling wave.

When it was done, blackness overcame him. He slept instantly, their bodies still joined.

Seventeen

The return trip to Charleston was so uneventful and anticlimactic that Jonathan wished they had chosen to finish their week in Antigua. He felt completely normal, but it was too late now.

The only holdup they experienced was at the airport in St. John's. They were forced to wait on the tarmac for an hour past their expected departure time, which meant it would be late afternoon when they touched down in Charleston, later still when they made it to the beach house.

It wasn't really a problem. Jonathan's father was away on a weeklong golf outing with his friends. Though the old man did little more than ride the cart, he enjoyed the company.

The housekeeper and chef had been summoned from their breaks. Jonathan would have to make it up to them later. In the meantime, the capable women would have dinner for four ready at six o'clock.

Jonathan and Lisette barely made it. They had both slept on the plane, and the trip had gone smoothly after the slow start. But the traffic in and around the Charleston airport when they exited at rush hour was heavy.

Neither of them spoke much on the drive out to the house. They were probably going to arrive just as Mazie and J.B. showed up.

Lisette pulled out a comb and compact, and fretted over her reflection.

He put a hand on her leg. "Relax. You look beautiful. It's just my sister."

"Easy for you to say. You're not the one who has crazy hair."

He managed a chuckle though his chest was tight. He dreaded telling Mazie and J.B. what had happened in Antigua.

In the end, both vehicles swept through the gate at almost the exact same instant. They parked and Jonathan took a deep breath. "Let's leave everything in the car until later."

Lisette nodded and squeezed his hand. "It will be okay. The truth is always better than secrets."

He wasn't entirely convinced, but he didn't really have a choice.

The four of them got out, exchanged hugs and climbed the front staircase. Once inside, fabulous smells wafted from the kitchen. Jonathan and Lisette had only snacked on the plane. And Jonathan had eaten sparingly at dinner the night before. His stomach growled audibly, making everyone laugh.

Mazie grinned at Lisette. "Didn't you feed him down in Antigua?"

Lisette grimaced. "You know your brother. He does his own thing."

Ordinarily they might have all enjoyed appetizers and drinks on the porch. As it was, since Jonathan was on an alcohol-free regimen, they went into the dining room at the housekeeper's suggestion so dinner could be served hot.

The meal was incredible, especially for such short notice. Seared scallops. A light corn chowder. Spinach salad and angel food cake with fresh strawberries for dessert.

Mazie was remarkably patient. She endured the conversation about sports and movies and whether or not the upcoming hurricane season was going to be a bad one. But as soon as the last dish was cleared away, she shifted her chair back from the table, pinned Jonathan with a challenging gaze, and wrapped her arms around her waist. "Okay, big brother. Tell me what happened. Why did your honeymoon get cut short?"

Lisette's heart went out to Jonathan. He was stone-faced, trapped by his sister's interrogation. Lisette was positive that if he'd had his way, no one would ever have known what happened out on that boat. No one but Lisette.

When he didn't say anything at first, she tried to deflect the attention from her silent husband. "We had an incident," she said, trying her best to downplay what had happened. But the facts were damning, and the other two adults at the table weren't stupid.

J.B. frowned. "What kind of incident?"

Jonathan stared out the window, his jaw tight. The tension in the room was desperately uncomfortable.

Lisette tried again. "Jonathan experienced severe pain behind his right eye. It affected his vision for a number of hours."

J.B. cursed under his breath. Mazie, predictably, started to cry.

Jonathan stood, rounded the table and put his arms around his sister from behind, kissing her cheek. "Don't make a thing of this, sis. I'm fine now."

His assurance was cold comfort.

Lisette had had over a day to get used to the idea that Jonathan might be incapacitated sooner rather than later. His sister and brother-in-law had not.

J.B. leaped to his feet and paced, his body language communicating his turmoil. "You know you'll have to use a driver, right? You can't take chances."

Lisette expected Jonathan to reply angrily, but his half smile was resigned. "I know. We'll deal with it."

Before anyone could say another word, the house-keeper appeared in the doorway. Lisette didn't know how much the woman had overhead, but she clearly hadn't wanted to interrupt.

"There's a car at the front gate, Mr. Tarleton. A Dr. Shapiro? He says he needs to speak to you. It's urgent."

Jonathan paled beneath his tan. "Buzz him in."

A deadly silence fell around the table. Then something clicked for Lisette. She looked at Jonathan. He's not your doctor…is he?"

"No." Jonathan shrugged. "I can't imagine what he wants."

A dozen scenarios flashed through Lisette's imagination, each one worse than the last. Maybe the cancer was further along than they had been led to believe. Jonathan's family doctor was a general practitioner. This other doctor might have been sent to deliver the news.

When the housekeeper ushered the newcomer into the dining room, no one said a word. The man was in his early sixties. Distinguished. Only a sprinkle of silver at his temples.

Jonathan stuck out his hand. "Dr. Shapiro? I don't think we've met. I'm Jonathan Tarleton. Call me Jonathan."

The older man wasted no time. "I'm the senior administrator at the hospital. May we speak in private, Jonathan? It's a matter of some urgency."

Jonathan's pallor increased. He looked around the room. "This is my family. They can hear whatever you have to say."

The doctor hesitated, clearly ill at ease. "Very well. There's no way to dance around this, so I'll just say it. You don't have cancer. There's no brain tumor."

All the oxygen was sucked out of the room by the incredible pronouncement.

"How do you know?" Jonathan's question was sharp.

Dr. Shapiro took a breath. "Our senior radiologist has been removed from the hospital's roster. His credentials have been revoked by the state licensing board. For the past two years he has been abusing prescription drugs and other substances. He took on more and more cases, and in the process, misread or transposed results."

Jonathan spoke sharply. "So I'm not the only one involved?"

The other man winced. "Many patients have been affected, though none with such grave results as yours. Part of it was financial. The radiologist was billing insurance and siphoning off cash. He has incorrectly read and reported on dozens if not hundreds of test results. Yours was one case out of many."

Mazie frowned. "I don't understand. How could he rise to the level of senior staff under these circumstances?"

"He was one of our best. But apparently, he's had some untreated issues of his own. His wife left him three years ago. That led to his recent downward spiral. I'm very sorry."

Lisette's brain struggled to do the math, and something didn't add up. "But you're not here to deliver good news, are you? That's why you're not smiling." Her heart was beating so rapidly in her chest she thought she might faint. When she went to Jonathan and slipped her hand into his, her husband's fingers were icy.

Dr. Shapiro's expression grew grimmer still. "Your recent test results did confirm a serious problem. But it's not either of the things you were told. You have a large brain aneurysm, Jonathan. As far as we can tell, it's been leaking slowly. That accounts for the severe headaches that have come and gone."

Mazie took her brother's other hand. "But there's a cure, surely. This is better than cancer."

J.B. wrapped his arm around his wife protectively. "Easy, Maze. Let the man talk."

Still, Jonathan was silent. The four of them faced the unwelcome visitor.

Dr. Shapiro ignored everyone in the room but the patient. "You'll need surgery as soon as we can arrange it. A few more tests in the meantime, of course—just because now we know what we're looking for—but no time wasted."

Lisette bit down hard on her lower lip. "What's the big rush? It's been there a long time, right?"

The doctor glanced at her and then back at Jonathan. "It could rupture at any moment, son. In forty percent of cases, that event is fatal."

Jonathan stepped away from his circle of loved ones. "And if it's not fatal, I could end up comatose."

Dr. Shapiro winced. "Neurological damage is a distinct possibility. That's why we want to do surgery without delay. I've taken the liberty of contacting a specialist at Emory in Atlanta. He's willing to come if we can work around his schedule. You're young and otherwise healthy. Your prognosis should be positive. And of course—under the circumstances—the hospital will cover any and all associated costs not covered by your insurance."

J.B. scowled. "I hardly think money is the issue here. Criminal negligence is more like it."

Mazie, surprisingly, stepped up her game, appearing both calm and decisive. She kissed Jonathan and hugged Lisette. "You guys need time to talk. We'll get out of here and leave you alone. I'll text you first thing tomorrow. In the meantime, we're only a phone call away."

After they departed, Dr. Shapiro addressed Jonathan. "I'd like you to be at my office at ten in the morning. We'll go over all the options. Do you have any more questions at the moment?"

Jonathan shook his head. "No. I'll be there."

Lisette shook the man's hand. "Thank you for coming in person. It means a lot."

The housekeeper showed the doctor to the door. Jonathan prowled the dining room, his expression thunderous. "Of course he came in person. They're about to get sued by dozens of families. He's doing damage control."

"That's not helping," Lisette said.

"You know what would help?"

"What?"

"Having sex with my wife."

Jonathan loved the fact that he could still make her blush.

She nodded slowly. "If you're sure you feel like it."

"I feel fine," he muttered. "That's the hell of it. C'mon. Let's get our stuff out of the car and go to bed."

By the time they grabbed their suitcases, the housekeeper and chef were finished in the kitchen. The two women bade them good-night. Jonathan locked up the house.

Outwardly, he was trying to act as if everything was normal. The reason for Lisette to be his wife had disappeared in an instant. No longer did he have to dread months of dwindling health. Either he recovered, or he would be gone.

Could he tell her he loved her? That he wanted to get her pregnant…to become a family for real? What would she say? Her deepest thoughts were still a mystery to him. He knew she cared about him at some level. She had a huge heart. But if he had this surgery and survived, would she want to stay?

The prospect filled him with jittery anticipation. He no longer faced a death sentence. There was a decent chance he was going to make a full recovery. For the first time in forever, he felt hope and jubilation effervesce in his chest.

He and Lisette went upstairs. It dawned on him halfway down the hall that tonight was another first. Lisette had never slept with him at the beach house.

He paused in the doorway to the bedroom and sighed. "Well, damn."

Lisette peeked around his shoulder and groaned.

Jonathan's walk-in closet was enormous, though he used barely a third of it. He had charged the assistant housekeeper and her teenage daughter with moving all of Lisette's personal belongings from her condo to her new residence. Obviously the two women had assumed they had the rest of the week to accomplish the task. Jonathan had forgotten to let them know about the change in plans.

At the moment, the big king-size bed was covered with stacks of Lisette's clothes that had been carried over from *her* closet.

Lisette elbowed past him and set down her bags. "No worries. We can just hang it all up, and I can organize later. It won't take us fifteen minutes."

She was right. They grabbed one pile at a time and hung garments on the empty rods. Jonathan had longer arms. He was able to take more with each trip. But near the end, he got too ambitious. A few things that were still in plastic dry-cleaning bags caused everything to shift, and he lost the lot of it on the floor.

He waved Lisette away. "I've got this. Go unpack your bag. Get ready for bed."

As he scooped up two hangars at a time, a white envelope fell out of a skirt pocket. He picked it up, ready to lay it aside, when he realized his name was neatly printed on the front. In Lisette's handwriting.

Curious, he opened the flap and scanned the letter. Everything inside him went icy cold. *She had been planning to leave him, to leave Tarleton Shipping.* He looked at the date on the letter. *This* was why he had found her in his office that fateful day. While he'd been reeling from his diagnosis, Lisette had been taking steps to change her life, to move on.

Despite his pretext of needing a decision maker in the office—someone to help him keep his illness a se-cret—he knew now that he had asked her to marry him because he'd been falling in love with her. He had believed there was a good chance she had feelings for him, too. Everything about their honeymoon had con-vinced him it was true.

After they slept together for the first time, he'd as-sumed the reason she'd accepted his outlandish proposal was because she wanted to explore the connection they shared. To be with him for whatever time he had left.

The truth was far worse. She had married him out of pity. Her compassionate heart and giving nature had convinced her to be his convenient wife, though the setup was *inconvenient* for her.

His stomach curled with nausea. If he truly loved her, he would have to let her go. She'd spent years of her adulthood caring for her mother. Judging from the letter, she had been on the verge of finally making a life that was her own. He sure as hell didn't want her to give up anything else for him.

Because he couldn't quite process this new informa-tion in the wake of everything else that had happened today, he shoved the letter into his pocket. He would deal with it later. When he knew what it was he wanted to say to her.

When she walked out of the bathroom wearing noth-ing but an Isle of Palms T-shirt with tiny bikini panties, her smile erased some of the ice encasing his heart. "Thanks for finishing that," she said.

His body tightened. Despite his stress and mental fatigue, the rest of him was raring to go. "No problem. Let me grab a quick shower and I'll meet you under the covers."

Her smile faltered. "Don't we need to talk about tomorrow? The doctor? Everything he said? You've had a shock, Jonathan."

Two shocks, he thought, remembering the letter. "To be honest, I'd rather have sex and then sleep with my wife. Tomorrow will come soon enough. I've had about all the bad news I can handle at the moment."

As if on cue, her cell phone rang. It was on the dresser. He was the closest, so he picked it up to hand it to her. The caller ID on the screen was like a punch to the gut. Hartley Tarleton.

Jonathan felt weird. Like his body was heavy but the rest of him was floating above the room, observing. He stared at Lisette. "Why the hell is my brother calling you?"

Her ringtone was a familiar Beatle's lyric about love being the only thing a person needed. It went on and on. She'd been holding out her hand for the phone. Now her arm dropped to her side. She was dead white, her gaze anxious. "I can explain."

He hit the button that denied the call. Now the silence was deafening. "No," he said carefully. "I don't believe you can."

The enormity of the betrayal sliced through him with a pain greater than what had happened to him on the boat. Lisette knew how he felt about Hartley. Everyone in his family knew.

She wrung her hands, the action oddly ludicrous. "I put his name in my list of contacts so I would know never to answer that number."

"Try again." His hands and his arms were numb. Was he having a heart attack? First Dr. Shapiro. Next, a jubilant moment when he thought all his dreams could come true. Then finding the letter. Now this.

Lisette lifted her chin. "He called me yesterday in Antigua. Hartley said he knew something was wrong with you…that you brothers had always shared a weird twin connection. I told him I couldn't talk to him. I didn't give him any information about you, I swear. I hung up as quickly as I could."

"I see." He studied her words. His brain was doing some kind of hyper supercomputer thing. Maybe Lisette was involved with Hartley somehow. And Jonathan had been stupid enough to sign a generous prenup, giving Lisette far more than Hartley had stolen from the company. What the hell was going on?

His bride stared at him. Tears brimmed in her eyes and rolled down her cheeks. "It's the truth. I swear." She swallowed visibly. "I love you, Jonathan. Let me help you. Don't push me away."

Let me help you.

"I don't need help," he said carefully. He no longer knew what to believe. But ultimately, her involvement with Hartley—or lack of—was a peripheral matter. Jonathan had to set her free. He couldn't let her sacrifice her life for his. If the only way he could push her away convincingly was to be harsh, he would do it, no matter how much it might hurt. He pulled the letter out of his pocket. "Remember this?"

"Oh, God."

"Indeed." He laid her resignation letter on the dresser. "I'm going to a hotel right now. When I get back tomorrow, I want you gone."

Lisette's face was ashen. "I know things have changed," she said. "But you married me to protect the company. We shouldn't be hasty. Let's take time to think things through."

"The reason I married you no longer exists. Either the surgery kills me—in which case my sister will take over all the decision making—or I'll recover and life will go on. But you have no place here. Not anymore."

"I told you I love you," she cried. "You have to believe me."

He shook his head slowly. "I don't know what to believe right now. Apparently nothing in my life is what it seems. I'm dissolving our arrangement, Lisette." He picked up the letter, his chest tight with despair. "Feel free to *pursue other opportunities* and *find new challenges*. It makes no difference at all to me," he lied. "I have more important things to worry about than your happiness and your future. That's up to you, I'm afraid." He heard the cold, cutting words leave his lips and watched them hit their mark.

Lisette trembled so hard her teeth were chattering. "I told you I love you. I want to be with you when you undergo this surgery. Please, Jonathan."

"No." He didn't dress it up.

She sucked in a deep breath, her gaze shattered. "Are you saying you want an annulment…a divorce?"

There would never be a baby. Not now. Knowing that was the most terrible blow of all.

"A divorce would be for the best. But we'll hit Pause

on the details until after the surgery. After all, this whole mess may sort itself out if my brain explodes."

"Don't say that," she cried.

He shrugged. "You heard the doctor. Forty percent fatal. The way my luck has been going lately, even I wouldn't place money on *my* chances."

"Please don't go," she begged. "Come to bed with me. You'll feel better in the morning."

The giant wall broke, the one that had been damming up all the pain and screaming regret in his gut. He felt it drag him under, knew the moment he reached his breaking point.

She wasn't his to keep, never had been.

"No thanks, Lizzy. I'm done with you."

Four days after Jonathan Tarleton kicked her out of his house, Lisette paced the floors of the hospital surgical wing. Waiting. Waiting. She had company. Mazie and J.B. were there, too, but they were huddled together in the family lounge, promising each other that Mazie's brother and Jonathan's best friend was going to make it.

Thinking about the surgery made Lisette ill. Somewhere nearby a surgeon was drilling a hole in her husband's skull, attempting to clip off the blood supply to the bulging pocket in a vessel or an artery. The specifics were hazy. She had tried to research the procedure, but the information she found had been so terrifying she decided ignorance was the best choice for now.

Because Jonathan had been adamant about his decision to exclude Lisette, she had been forced to tell Mazie everything. Thankfully, J.B.'s and Mazie's kindness had soothed the edges of her wretched heartbreak.

Still, as soon as Jonathan was conscious, she would

no longer be able to hang around. The thought was unbearable.

The more she thought about it, though, the more determined she became to ignore his edict. Jonathan was only half of this relationship. She had a right to fight for him, and she would. For a brief moment in Antigua, happiness had been in her grasp.

She would get it back if she had to beat the stupid man over the head. He loved her. She had to believe that. His body had told her so again and again, even if he hadn't managed the actual words.

At long last, the surgery was over and Jonathan was moved to ICU.

Mazie's red-rimmed eyes telegraphed relief. "You go in first," she said. "He's out of it, and it will make you feel better."

Lisette hugged her tightly. "Thank you." She slipped into the curtained cubicle and felt her heart shatter all over again. Jonathan looked so alone. So very far away. They had shaved a small section of his head, she knew that. A white bandage covered the wound.

Carefully she pulled the single small chair closer to the side of the bed. She picked up the large male hand that wasn't tethered to an IV. Curling her fingers around his, she spoke to him softly.

"It's me, Jonathan. Lizzy. Your wife. I know we played a charade, but I so badly wanted it to be real. I've loved you forever, it seems. When I thought you were dying, I didn't know how I would go on. I decided I wanted to be with you for however long we had together. Now you're angry and hurt, and I don't know what to do. If you can hear me, please listen. You are mine, you stubborn man. I adore you, and I'm pretty sure you love me, too. I want to make a baby with you and a future. So I'm not letting you go."

She wanted to say more, but tears clogged her throat. Mazie had been generous to give her this time. Mazie and J.B. would want to come in, too.

When she thought she could leave without embarrassing herself, she wiped her face and stood. All around her, machines beeped and whooshed. Jonathan lay still as death, not entirely out of the woods.

Here and now, she resolved to fight. It would require patience and waiting for the right moment to help him see the truth. Not only that, she might have to play hardball to make him admit that he loved her. Maybe a little subterfuge on her part.

All's fair in love and war…

Though it took every bit of strength she could muster, she walked out of his room, out of the hospital—but not out of his life.

Eighteen

One month later...

Jonathan stood in front of Lisette's condo and knocked carefully. His recovery had moved far too slowly for his satisfaction. And there had been bumps in the road. Today was the first time he'd been allowed behind the wheel of a car. And only now because he had told his sister he needed to see his wife.

When Lisette opened the door, he drank in the sight of her. Her face was thinner, her gaze guarded. She didn't seem too surprised. Maybe Mazie had tipped her off.

"Hello, Lisette," he said.

"Come in." She stepped back and waited for him to walk toward the living room.

In the arched doorway, he jerked back, startled.

There were moving boxes stacked neatly in two corners. "You're leaving? I thought you loved this condo."

Lisette sat down in a chair and motioned for him to do the same. "I'm moving to Savannah. I have three job interviews lined up next week."

He was stunned. What had he expected? That she was going to wait on him to quit being a giant pain in the ass? Her announcement left him off script and reeling.

When he couldn't come up with a response to her news, she pointed to a small pile on the coffee table. "The wedding band and engagement ring are in the boxes. Your lawyer drew up papers nullifying our prenup. I've signed everything. All you have to do is add your signature and file the documents. I cleaned out my desk at work and turned in keys. If I've forgotten anything, feel free to text me."

At last he found his voice. "You can't dissolve the prenup without my consent."

"Actually, I can. The agreement was predicated on your diagnosis of terminal cancer. Since that no longer applied, everything else was off the table. Your lawyer agreed, but of course, feel free to discuss it with her."

"And what about your termination package from Tarleton Shipping?"

Her eyelids flickered as though his barb had hit some unseen mark. "I turned in my original resignation letter. I wasn't entitled to severance."

He gripped the arms of the chair, trying not to grab her up and kiss her until her calm facade cracked. "I'm sorry, Lizzy. So damned sorry. That night we returned from our honeymoon was a terrible time in my life…

even worse than the day they told me I had cancer. I wasn't myself. Please forgive me."

She stared at the rug. "Nothing to forgive. You were in shock. It's understandable."

"I love you," he said, feeling desperate because she was slipping away. Irrevocably.

This time she looked straight at him, but it was as if she hadn't heard what he said. "You should know that I've talked to Hartley multiple times in the last few weeks. He's been extremely worried about you, and I thought he should have as much information as possible."

Jonathan blinked. The old feelings of anger and betrayal tried to take hold. "I don't know why my brother did what he did, but I won't be batshit crazy about it anymore. Looking death in the face has a way of rearranging a man's priorities."

"I'm glad to know that. I hope the two of you can reconcile some day."

"Did you hear me?" Jonathan said hoarsely. "I told you I love you."

She shook her head slowly. Those translucent green eyes held pain he had put there. "You've had plenty of opportunities to tell me that over the years and you never said it. Even on our honeymoon when we were as close as two people can be, you didn't say it. You liked having sex with me. I know that. But it's two different things."

He stood up, no longer able to contain his nervous energy. "I do love you," he said. "The only reason I didn't say anything earlier was because I thought you would grieve more when I was gone if you knew."

"That's an interesting theory," she said, her smile

more wry than sarcastic. "You're a closed-off man, Jonathan. Aloof. Afraid of letting anyone get close. You love your sister and your father and J.B., but even with them, you didn't want to share the news that you had cancer. You wanted to handle everything on your own. The only person who has ever really known you intimately is your twin brother. And now you've locked him out of your life, too."

"I asked *you* for help."

She shook her head slowly. "Only because you saw me as an uninterested bystander. You thought I could be impartial. Unbiased. You needed me to be a buffer between you and the rest of the world."

"It's not true." He scraped his hands through his hair, his fingers brushing unwittingly over the bumpy scar that would always be a reminder. "Okay, maybe I told you that. I may have even thought I believed it. But in Antigua, I let myself see the real you. I wasn't your boss anymore. I was your lover." He hesitated. "Do you remember that day on the boat?"

Lisette's eyes widened as if aghast he would bring it up. "Of course I remember it," she said. "It was the best moment of our trip, right up until it wasn't. But I'm not sure why we're rehashing the details. You could have died in front of me. I've never been so terrified."

"I can't forget, either," he said slowly, pausing at the window but not really seeing the view. "I watched you sitting in the bow of the boat…laughing, beautiful, so damned happy. I knew then that I loved you. Whether you believe me or not, I decided that when we got home I was going to try one more time to see if there were any last-ditch treatments. Any hope at all."

He turned to face her. "I wanted to fight, Lizzy. Because I realized I loved you. When Dr. Shapiro told us the truth, I knew you and I had a chance."

"But then you found my letter."

He grimaced. "It was bad timing all the way around. I had admitted to myself that I loved you, but suddenly I realized you had sacrificed a portion of your life for me out of what appeared to be duty or compassion. I wanted to set you free. So I deliberately pushed you away."

He'd given it his all, every ounce of truth. He'd put his heart on the line. But nothing in her expression changed. If anything, she had retreated into herself. Perhaps she learned that move from him.

"Say something," he demanded.

"It doesn't matter," she said softly, her eyes shiny with tears. "Think back, Jonathan. You loved your life before you got sick. You adored the pressure-cooker environment, and you relished being in charge. You seldom dated, because you didn't have the time to give to a relationship. Your future was all mapped out, and you liked it."

"I liked it because you were there with me."

She inhaled sharply. "I can't be that woman anymore. Things have changed."

He crossed the room in two strides and pulled her to her feet, gripping her hands tightly. "Then I'll change, too. The night I was so cruel to you, you said you loved me. Is it not true anymore? Is that one of the changes my selfishness caused?"

Lisette had used up her last reserves of courage. When Mazie told her Jonathan was coming to see her, it seemed like a personal challenge. Was she going to fight for him? She was tired of making sacrifices for other people, tired of hiding her feelings.

The moving ruse was a way to needle him, but if things didn't work out, it would become a reality.

The past month had seemed like a desert journey. She had grieved the loss of Jonathan endlessly…had scrounged for any tiny scraps of information about his recovery.

When he was dismissed from the hospital, it was even worse. Then all she could do was imagine him out at the beach house, sleeping in the bed that was supposed to be theirs.

Now here he was, saying things and doing things that were too enchanting to be true.

"Maybe I love you, and maybe I don't," she said. "But if you're here out of guilt —if that's all it is— you can go back to being you. I deserve to be happy. I deserve a man who cares more about his wife and his family than his need to be in control of everything."

He searched her face. "That man is gone. I wouldn't take him back, even if he came crawling. When I was in the hospital, I had to learn how to accept help. How to be grateful to doctors and nurses who were doing their damnedest to keep me alive. I wasn't in charge, Lisette. I wasn't top dog. I like to think I learned a bit of humility. But if I brag about it too much, it kind of defeats the purpose," he joked.

She stared at him, only now realizing that a new light shone from his eyes, a new peace.

He rubbed his thumb over her cheek. "Please, my love. Tell me you don't love me if that's what you want to say, but you're going to have to work to make me believe it. Because I remember what it was like to be inside you when you screamed my name. I still hear those moments in my dreams."

Her joy and her fear collided in her chest. "My period is three weeks late," she blurted out. "You didn't sign on for that."

He stared at her, trying to process the incredible words. He put a hand on her flat belly. "Of course I did. It was my idea on the boat that day, remember?"

"But only because you thought it would be all up to me later. You thought you were going to be dead and gone. Parenting is two decades or more of flat-out hard work."

He dropped his forehead to hers, his whole body shaking. "I adore you, Lizzy Tarleton. There's nothing in this world I would like more than to make a dozen babies with you and live happily ever after."

Lisette sobbed, wiping her cheek on his shoulder. "Truly?" Was this terrible nightmare really over?

He pulled her close. "We said vows. For better or for worse. We've gotten the latter out of the way early. Now let's plan our future together, my love." He scooped her up and sat on the sofa with her in his lap. "And you might want to stop crying, because I bought this new shirt just for today."

Her giggle was watery.

He bent his head and kissed her. Lisette wrapped her arms around his neck. "I do love you, Jonathan," she whispered. "I've loved you for a very long time. But…"

He reared back, alarm written on his face. "But what?"

"I think three babies will be enough."

His smile returned. "I'll wear you down."

She felt his sex pressing beneath her leg and knew that he wanted her every bit as much as she wanted him. "How do you feel about make-up sex?" she asked, stroking his bottom lip suggestively.

His grin was devilishly masculine and enthusiastic. "I thought you'd never ask."

* * * * *

Hartley Tarleton reveals his own secrets— and the ones his family has been hiding for decades—in the searing conclusion to the Southern Secrets trilogy.

Available October 2019!

#2665 HIS TO CLAIM
The Westmoreland Legacy • by Brenda Jackson
Honorary Westmoreland Thurston "Mac" McRoy delayed a romantic ranch vacation with his wife for too long—she went without him! Now it will take all his skills to rekindle their desire and win back his wife...

#2666 RANCHER IN HER BED
Texas Cattleman's Club: Houston • by Joanne Rock
Rich rancher Xander Currin isn't looking for a relationship. Cowgirl Frankie Walsh won't settle for anything less. When combustible desire consumes them both just as secrets from Frankie's past come to light, will their passion survive?

#2667 TAKEN BY STORM
Dynasties: Secrets of the A-List • by Cat Schield
Isabel Withers knows her boss, hotel executive Shane Adams, should be off-limits—but the chances he'll notice her are zilch. Until they're stranded together in a storm and let passion rule. Can their forbidden love overcome the scandals waiting for them?

#2668 THE BILLIONAIRE'S BARGAIN
Blackout Billionaires • by Naima Simone
Chicago billionaire Darius King never surrenders...until a blackout traps him with an irresistible beauty. Then the light reveals his enemy—his late best friend's widow! Marriage is the only way to protect his friend's legacy, but soon her secrets will force Darius to question everything...

#2669 FROM MISTAKE TO MILLIONS
Switched! • by Andrea Laurence
A DNA kit just proved Jade Nolan is *not* a Nolan. Desperate for answers, she accepts the help of old flame Harley Dalton—even though she knows she can't resist him. What will happen when temptation leads to passion and the truth complicates everything?

#2670 STAR-CROSSED SCANDAL
Plunder Cove • by Kimberley Troutte
When Chloe Harper left Hollywood to reunite with her family, she vowed to heal herself before hooking up with *anyone*. But now sexy star-maker Nicolas Medeiros is at her resort, offering her the night of her dreams. She takes it...and more. But how will she let him go?

SPECIAL EXCERPT FROM

HQN™

*Beatrix Leighton has loved Gold Valley cowboy
Dane Parker from afar for years, and she's about to
discover that forbidden love might just be the sweetest...*

Read on for a sneak preview of
Unbroken Cowboy
by New York Times *and* USA TODAY
bestselling author Maisey Yates.

It was her first kiss. But that didn't matter.

It was Dane. That was all that mattered. That was all that really mattered.

Dane, the man she'd fantasized about a hundred times—maybe a thousand times—doing this very thing. But this was so much brighter and more vivid than a fantasy could ever be. Color and texture and taste. The rough whiskers on his face, the heat of his breath, the way those big, sure hands cupped her face as his lips moved slowly over hers.

She took a step and the shattered glass crunched beneath her feet, but she didn't care. She didn't care at all. She wanted to breathe in this moment for as long as she could, broken glass be damned. To exist just like this, with his lips against hers, for as long as she possibly could.

She leaned forward, wrapped her fingers around the fabric of his T-shirt and clung to him, holding them both steady, because she was afraid she might fall if she didn't.

Her knees were weak. Like in a book or a movie.

She hadn't known that kissing could really, literally, make your knees weak. Or that touching a man you wanted could make you feel like you were burning up, like you had a fever. Could make you feel hollow and restless and desperate for what came next...

Even if what came next scared her a little.

It was Dane.

She trusted Dane.

With her secrets. With her body.

Dane.

She breathed his name on a whispered sigh as she moved to take their kiss deeper, and found herself being set back, glass crunching beneath her feet yet again.

"I should go," he said, his voice rough.

"No!" The denial burst out of her, and she found herself reaching forward to grab his shirt again. "No," she said again, this time a little less crazy and desperate.

She didn't feel any less crazy and desperate.

"I have to go, Bea."

"You don't. You could stay."

The look he gave her burned her down to the soles of her feet. "I can't."

"If you're worried about… I didn't misunderstand. I mean I know that if you stayed we would…"

"Dammit, Bea," he bit out. "We can't. You know that."

"Why? I'm not stupid. I know you don't want… I don't want…" She stumbled over her words because it all seemed stupid. To say something as inane as she knew they wouldn't get married. Even saying it made her feel like a silly virgin.

She was a virgin. There wasn't really any glossing over that. But she didn't have to seem silly.

She did know, though. For all that everyone saw her as soft and naive, she wasn't. She'd carried a torch for Dane for a long time but she'd also realistically seen how marriage worked. Her brother was a cheater. Her mother was a cheater.

Her father was… She didn't even know.

That was the legacy of love and marriage in her family.

Truly, she didn't want any part of it.

Some companionship, though. Sex. She wanted that. With him. Why couldn't she have that? McKenna made it sound simple, and possible. And Bea wanted it.

Don't miss
Unbroken Cowboy *by Maisey Yates,*
available May 2019 wherever Harlequin® books
and ebooks are sold.

www.Harlequin.com

*Honorary Westmoreland Thurston "Mac" McRoy
delayed a romantic ranch vacation with his wife for too
long—she went without him! Now it will take all his
skills to rekindle their desire and win back his wife…*

Read on for a sneak peek at
His to Claim
by New York Times *bestselling author Brenda Jackson!*

Thurston McRoy, called Mac by all who knew him, still had
his arms around his mother's shoulders when he felt her tense
up. "Mom? You okay?" he asked, looking down at her.

When his parents glanced over at each other, that uneasy
feeling from earlier crept over him again. Not liking it, he
turned to go down the hall toward his bedroom when his father
reached out to stop him.

"Teri isn't here, Mac."

Mac turned back to his father. His mother had moved to
stand beside his dad.

"It's after two in the morning and tomorrow is a school day
for the girls. So where is she?"

His mother reached out and touched his arm. "She needed
to get away and she asked if we would come keep the girls."

Mac frowned. He knew his wife. She would not have gone
anywhere without their daughters. "What do you mean, she
needed to get away? Why?"

"She's the one who has to tell you that, Thurston. It's not
for us to say."

Mac drew in a deep breath, not understanding any of this. Because his parents were acting so secretive, he felt his confusion and anger escalating. "Fine. Where is she?"

It was his father who spoke. "She left three days ago for the Torchlight Dude Ranch."

Mac's frown deepened. "The Torchlight Dude Ranch? In Wyoming?"

"Yes."

"What the hell did she go there for?"

His father didn't say anything for a minute and then gave Mac an answer. "She said she always wanted to go back there."

Mac rubbed his hand across his face. Yes, Teri had always wanted to go back there, the place he'd taken her on their honeymoon, a little over ten years ago. And he'd always promised to take her back. But between his covert missions and their growing family, there had never been enough time. Teri, who'd been raised on a ranch in Texas, was a cowgirl at heart and had once dreamed of being on the rodeo circuit due to her roping and riding skills. She'd even represented the state of Texas as a rodeo queen years ago.

When they'd married, she had given it all up to travel around the world with her naval husband. She'd said she'd done so gladly. Why in the world would Teri leave their kids and go to a dude ranch by herself?

He knew the only person who could answer that question was Teri.

It was time to go find his wife.

His to Claim
by New York Times *bestselling author Brenda Jackson,*
available June 2019 wherever
Harlequin® Desire books and ebooks are sold.

www.Harlequin.com

  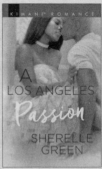
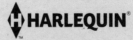